A Nose for Adventure

A Nose for Adventure

Richard Scrimger

Tundra Books

Published in Canada by Tundra Books,
McClelland & Stewart Young Readers,
481 University Avenue, Toronto, Ontario M5G 2E9

Published in the United States by Tundra Books of Northern New York,
P.O. Box 1030, Plattsburgh, New York 12901

Library of Congress Control Number: 00-131578

Canadian Cataloguing in Publication Data

Scrimger, Richard, 1957-
A nose for adventure

ISBN 0-88776-499-1

I. Title.

PS8587.C745N674 2000 jC813'.54 C00-930680-3
PZ7.S37No 2000

We acknowledge the support of the Canada Council for the Arts and the Ontario Arts Council for our publishing program.

We acknowledge the financial support of the Government of Canada through the Book Publishing Industry Development Program for our publishing activities.

Design by Ingrid Paulson
Illustration by Gillian Johnson

Printed and bound in Canada

2 3 4 5 6 05 04 03 02 01

For C. E. and especially T. I. D.

Acknowledgments

Many people contributed to *A Nose for Adventure.* Let me take the opportunity to thank Kathy Lowinger, who arm wrestled me into writing a better ending; Sue Tate, who smoothly and gracefully negotiated problems of clarity and continuity; and Marthe Jocelyn, whose encouragement and New York insights were vital.

And, of course, I mustn't ignore my regular support system: Dean and the rest of the agency, Bridget and the rest of the family.

Finally, and in a way most important of all, I'd like to thank all the readers of *The Nose from Jupiter.* Without you, there wouldn't be a sequel.

1

My Stomach, Lost and Lonely

The plane lurches sharply, leaving my stomach behind. I hate that feeling. I look out the window on my right, half expecting to see my stomach hurrying after me to catch up. I see clouds up close, wisps of gray, and then sky – nothing but sky for miles in all directions, including down. I think about crashing. I think about my stomach, lost and lonely without me, floating in midair, full of orange juice and breakfast cereal. These thoughts don't make me feel better. I groan.

"Stop that," says the girl beside me.

It's my first airplane trip all by myself. All alone. My mom is hiking in the woods with a group of troubled kids from work. My dad is waiting at the airport for my plane to land.

I hope we land. I hope he's waiting. I check my pants pocket for the American quarter my mom put there. "This is your emergency quarter," she told me, frowning fiercely, buttoning up my pocket herself. I'm thirteen; I hate it when she does stuff like that. "If your father isn't there when the plane lands, call him, and yell at him for me. Okay?"

My fingers touch the quarter, and the slip of paper with the phone number of my dad's office. I'm starting to feel better. I take a deep breath, and try to relax. And then the plane swoops down. I'm in row 17 – I figure my stomach is back around row 24. I groan again.

"Shut up, will you, kid," says the girl beside me. Her name is Frieda Miller. She's fourteen, a year older than me. She's seen it all. I told her my name – Alan – but she just laughed and called me kid.

"You sound like you're going to be sick," she says. "Are you?" Her hand is on the armrest between our seats. She has scarred knuckles and thick strong fingers.

I don't say anything.

"Are you going to be sick, kid?" she asks. "Your face is a weird yellowy green color. You'd better hang on to your airsick bag. Keep your head down. Don't turn it this way. I don't want you to be sick on my new pantsuit. It's a designer original."

If I turn that way, I'll be looking at her. Of course I don't do it.

She laughs. "Yellowy green, like the stripes on your stupid shirt. And you're sweating. You sure look funny."

She's chewing minty gum. I can smell it. How can Frieda

be so calm? The plane is diving around like a swallow after mosquitoes. My stomach makes its way slowly back towards my row, then the plane banks into a tight turn, and we drift apart again. The ground – actually, the skyscrapers of New York – appear in the window.

"Where did you get that shirt, anyway?" Frieda asks. "It's too big. Is it your dad's? And why does it have a picture of a donut on it?"

I don't answer.

Poor Dad, he'll probably be upset if we crash. I'm his only child, after all, even though he and Mom are divorced and we only see each other in the summer. Our local radio station back home will make a big deal of it too: *Among those believed killed in the New York City plane disaster is Cobourg's own Alan Dingwall.*

My ears are tight enough to explode. Then they do. Ouch.

Veronica wanders by. She's a special flight attendant who's been assigned to Frieda and me, seeing as we're kids flying on our own. Veronica has a great big smile on her face all the time, even when she's not talking about happy things. Like now. "We're going down," she says, smiling happily. "Going down now."

Down! That's why my ears are popping. I try to stay calm, but I don't succeed. "AAAAGH!" I shout. "No! NO! No! Why? Why me?!"

The passengers across the aisle are looking over.

Frieda pats me on the arm. Her grin is wide and mean. Her teeth are white. "She means we're landing, stupid," she says.

"What?" Did I hear right? My ears pop some more. My heart is pounding. "We're not crashing?" I say to Veronica. "We're going to live?"

Veronica smiles and nods. "You're going to be fine," she says. "Would you like some gum?" Her smile seems separate from her face. Like a mask. I wonder if she takes it off at night before going to bed.

"Sure," I say.

"I have my own," says Frieda.

Veronica gives me some gum and walks away.

"Want to arm wrestle again?" asks Frieda.

"Nope." My arm aches from the last time.

"Come on," she says. "I'll use my wrong arm. I'll use only two fingers. You still won't win, but the match will last longer. Come on!"

I shake my head.

Frieda's wheelchair falls over.

Frieda is not sitting in the wheelchair when it falls. She's in a regular airplane seat like me. But she's usually in a wheelchair. Her legs don't work very well. They never have, not since she was born. She explained it to me when we sat down together at the start of the flight. Actually, she went on and on about it. I was too scared to pay much attention, but I was happy to hear her voice in the background, talking about muscles and bones that don't do what they should. Her legs are a mess, is about it. She's had a dozen operations to fix them, and they're still a mess. One of her doctors works at The Hospital for Sick Children in Toronto.

Frieda flies between New York and Toronto a lot. Her Aunt Mary Lee – I think that's what she said – lives in Toronto, and Frieda stays with her when she's getting checked out. She's flying home to New York City now.

Frieda hasn't explained why she's on the flight alone. Her dad is a New York state representative, whatever that is. Sounds important. Maybe that's why he's not on the flight with her. She hasn't mentioned her mom at all. Mostly, she's been making fun of me, talking about my clothes, my hair, where I live, the way I say words like "house" and "about" and "roof." Oh yes, and she's been beating me at arm wrestling. Frieda's strong – her forearms must be twice as thick around as mine.

It's been a lot of fun, sitting beside her.

We're up at the front of the plane, with a wall in front of us. When we were getting seated, Veronica folded the wheelchair up very carefully and stowed it against the wall. With all the swooping and sailing around we were doing right now, the straps that tied the chair in place must have loosened. Anyway, the wheelchair falls onto the rug in front of me.

I get out of my window seat and try to lift the chair back into position. It's heavy and awkward. Veronica comes up behind me and grabs my arm. Her fingers are white. She's squeezing hard. Ouch.

"Don't you see the sign?" she asks. "Keep your seat belt on at all times during the descent."

"Sorry," I say.

"He couldn't lift the chair anyway," says Frieda, with a sneer.

"The passengers, and their belongings, are my responsibility," Veronica says.

"Sure," I say, after a pause. Her smile looks real, but she's upset. "Whatever you say."

I climb back into my seat.

"Good," says Veronica.

Ladies and Gentlemen, this is your captain speaking.

The plane is pointing down. Out the window I see water. My ears pop. The plane corkscrews around again. My stomach is flattened against my spine. My eyeballs almost fall out.

We will be landing at La Guardia Airport in a couple of minutes. It's eight thirty, and a warm and cloudy summer morning in New York City. Thanks for flying Air Canada. We hope to see you again soon.

The water gets closer and closer. The engine noise, which is loud, gets even louder. I shut my eyes and think of Mom. And Dad at the airport. I think of Miranda, my . . . well, sort of girlfriend, who promised to write to me every day. And Victor, my best friend, who didn't. And then there's a bump and we start to roll. We're on the ground, and Frieda is yawning. My pulse slows. My eyeballs and stomach settle back where they belong.

The plane trip is over. I don't ever want to fly again. Unfortunately, I've got a return ticket.

We get off last. Frieda is in the wheelchair now, pushing herself forward. Her forearm muscles ripple. The wheelchair is gray leather and chrome tubing, with TREKKER

DELUXE on the side, and black plastic grip handles at the back. Veronica stays close beside it. I hold open the doors to the terminal building.

We pass crowds of people waiting to fly out of New York. We pass lines of people waiting to get their hand luggage X-rayed. I did all this back in Toronto, with Mom.

Frieda obviously knows the way. After we pass a line of people waiting to walk through a metal detector, she spins around in her chair and backs into a door marked PRIVATE. The door opens on a dingy hall with an elevator, which takes us down to the baggage pickup area. This is a big basement of a room, with conveyor belts of suitcases going around and around in tight circles.

Frieda pushes herself to the front of the crowd of waiting passengers. "Out of the way," she says, in a bored tone of voice, like she's done this millions of times. "Coming through."

I follow behind. My clothes are in an equipment bag, which is easy to spot because the team name is printed on the side in big white letters. I lean over, but mistime my reach. My bag slides away. Frieda snickers. When it comes around again, she reaches out one arm and hoists it up.

"It's the same colors as your shirt," she says with a laugh. "Who are the Commodores?"

"My soccer team," I say.

"Soccer," she says, disdainfully. "What a stupid game. Who'd want a soccer bag?"

I'm worried. I haven't seen my dad in months, and I'm going to be spending the next week with him. And I'm mad at Frieda. "Soccer players," I say, quietly. "And, well, the chess team doesn't get equipment bags."

Now I feel bad. Of course she doesn't play soccer. "Sorry," I say, blushing. With my red hair, a blush makes my whole head look like it's on fire. She turns away.

Frieda's luggage is taking awhile. Veronica's permanent smile is starting to show signs of wear. "Only fifteen minutes until nine o'clock," she says. She doesn't say what will happen at nine o'clock.

Across the room is a corridor with a sign that says WAY OUT.

"There it is." Frieda points to a brown and black leather suitcase with gold stitching. It looks like it cost a lot more than my soccer bag.

Veronica leans over the conveyor belt and grabs the suitcase. I pick up my bag. The WAY OUT corridor is in shadow. WAY OUT to what? My dad will be at the end of the corridor, waiting for me.

"Oh, look at the sweetie!" I think that's the first nice thing I've heard out of Frieda's mouth. She points to a police dog on a leash. The dog doesn't look like a sweetie to me. It looks tough and alert. It sits in one place, swiveling its head around, searching for bad guys. The policeman holding the dog's leash looks tough too – but not alert. His head is still. He's staring at nothing in particular. His uniform is different from the ones at home. He looks like a cop on TV.

"I'm not allowed to have a dog," says Frieda. "But I wish I could. Hi, sweetie!" she calls. The dog looks over, briefly, then goes back to work.

For a second she – Frieda, not the dog – gets this look of real longing on her face. I know the look. I get it too, sometimes. She wants a pet. She wants something to stroke and cuddle, something to talk to and play with. Something to love.

There's a desk beside the WAY OUT corridor. A tall thin guy stands behind it, frowning at us.

"Took your time," he says. "My shift ends at nine, you know."

"Sorry," says Veronica.

The tall thin guy wears a white shirt, with a crest on the pocket. He's holding a clipboard. "Baggage tags," he says, in a raspy voice.

Oh, yeah. Mom went over and over this with me. You can't take your baggage without a tag. I feel for mine in my pocket. Frieda already has her tag out. We hand them over. The skinny guy doesn't seem to care about my tag. He puts it in his pocket. But he stares at Frieda's, then at her suitcase.

"This doesn't match," he says. He has a long face and a long thin nose. His voice rasps like a file.

"Of course it does," she says.

He shows her the tag in his hand. It isn't even the right color.

"That's not the one I gave you," she says. "That's someone else's tag. You got it out of your pocket."

"I'm going to have to ask you some questions," he says.

"That's someone else's tag, I said."

"Are you an American citizen?"

He looks official. Clipboard and everything. If he were talking to me, I'd answer. Frieda doesn't. She raises her eyebrow. "It's a mistake!" she says. "Besides, we went through customs before we left Canada."

He makes a note on his clipboard. His fingers and fingernails are as long and thin as the rest of him. "Are you bringing anything in from Canada?" he says.

"But they asked already. . . ."

"Better answer," says Veronica. "Follow the routine. This kind of mistake has happened to me too."

Frieda sighs. "All right, all right. These Ancient Egyptian earrings," she says. "My aunt got them for me at the museum shop in Toronto."

"Ancient Egyptian?" He stares. I stare too. The earrings look like birds.

"Well, they're not real, course. They're copies. The hawk is the symbol of Horus."

We studied Ancient Egypt in school. "Horus the god?" I say, to let her know I know.

"No, Horus the dentist," she snaps. "Of course, Horus the god. You know a lot of other Horuses?"

"Horus!" His skinny nose twitches towards Veronica. "Isn't that –" He breaks off, shaking his head.

A tall tanned lady stalks towards us, dragging a suitcase on little wheels. She's wearing leopard sandals; her dark red toenails look like claws. She tosses her baggage tag onto the desk and stalks away. "Bureaucrats," she says, making it sound like a dirty word. I watch her all the way down the WAY OUT corridor.

My dad will be waiting at the other end of the corridor. He'll ask what the plane trip was like, and I'll say it was fine. I won't be able to tell him how scared I felt. He flies all the time; he wouldn't understand. Will he think my shirt and soccer bag are stupid? Probably not. He probably won't notice what I'm wearing.

The skinny guy puts down his clipboard. "And now I'm afraid we're going to have to search your chair – I mean, baggage," he says to Frieda. "Could you go into the blue room, please?" He points behind him. Halfway down the corridor is a small blue door with the sign: EMPLOYEES ONLY.

Frieda looks snooty. "You can't search my baggage," she says.

"I am a government employee." His raspy voice deepens. "I have all sorts of powers."

Sounds like he's Aquaman. He doesn't look the part at all.

"My father is a state representative," she says. "I've *never* been searched before."

"Don't worry," says Veronica. "It won't take long. I'll just take Alan to meet his father, and then I'll come and be with you."

"I don't need anyone to be with me," says Frieda. "I'll be fine. And I don't need to have my baggage searched by any government employee," she adds, glaring.

The conveyor belt goes around and around. The policeman leans against the wall, picking his teeth with the corner of a book of matches. I don't see the dog.

I grab my bag and make for the WAY OUT. Veronica doesn't have much to say to me, and I don't have anything to say to her. The noise gets louder. I feel like an athlete, going down the tunnel that leads from the dressing room to the stadium. I get past the blue door, reach the end of the corridor, and stop.

Not a stadium. It's too dingy, too narrow, too low. But is it ever busy! I see more people, probably, in five seconds, than there are in my whole home town. Thousands and thousands of them – walking quickly, talking quickly, hugging and handshaking, dodging each other like pinballs in a fast-moving arcade game. Even the hugs and handshakes happen fast. I get bumped into from behind by a passenger hurrying by me. He disappears into the moving crowd like a snowflake into a river.

I stand at the end of the corridor and stare around me with a strange feeling in the middle of my chest. Not my stomach this time. I can feel my heart sinking. I stare harder.

I see babies and toddlers and kids and teens and tough guys. I see movie stars and nuns and cowboys. I see people on holiday and on business – old people, sad people, poor people, rich people. I see a familiar face: the skinny guy. He hurries past me into the crowd. I guess his shift is over, and he's finished searching Frieda's luggage. I notice that he's left the blue door open behind him.

My heart sinks further, keeps sinking, and finally goes down for the third time. No matter how hard I look, I can't see my dad.

He's not waiting for me. That's what Mom's afraid of, and has been ever since Dad mentioned the trip to me. I fight down anxiety like a mouthful of cooked carrots. I hate cooked carrots.

2

Long Way from Nome

Dad was transferred a few months back. He used to work in Vancouver. When I got knocked unconscious, he flew all the way across the country to be with me. Now he has a new job. I can't remember the name of the town where he lives, but he takes the train to New York City every day. He called me last month to tell me all about it, and to invite me for a visit.

"How'd you like to see the Big Apple, hey, champ?" he asked me, his voice crackling with static interference. Champ is what he calls me when he's being enthusiastic. "You can fly down when you get out of school. We'll stay at a hotel for the week," he said, "go to a baseball game, order room service, run around town together, have a great time. What do you say, champ?"

I told him that sounded great. Especially the room service. Imagine picking up the phone and ordering a restaurant meal, and then eating it in front of the TV. Cooler than cool. I could hardly wait.

Mom didn't think it was great. She wanted Dad to fly with me. She and Dad had an argument when I got off the phone. I could hear them – Mom's side of it, anyway. Dad's side wasn't hard to figure out.

"You're so irresponsible," she said.

He said something back to her. I don't know what – something mean, probably. Her face tightened up.

"Oh, yes?" she said. "Remember that time in Muskoka, when I left you alone with him for two hours? Just two hours. . . ."

I don't like listening to my parents' arguments, even if I'm only getting one side of them. I especially don't like it when they drag up old grudges. I was a baby when we went to Muskoka.

I suppose Dad must have made some excuse. Mom snorted. "Okay, then, what about that time when you left the car keys in the car?"

I went upstairs at that point. I didn't want to hear any more.

I'm startled out of my daydream by a cry for help. I'm standing just inside the corridor. The door to the blue room is open.

"Hey!" cries Frieda, from inside the room. "Hey, what are you doing? Help!"

I hear a sound like someone clapping hands, then a deeper voice saying, "Police! What's going on, here?"

Unsure of what to do, I look for Veronica. She moves quickly towards the blue door, and throws it wide open. I stay close behind her.

The inside of the room is painted the same deep blue as the door. There's a table for checking baggage, a chair for sitting, and a desk for filling out forms. The lighting is harsh and unforgiving – kind of like the expression on Frieda's face.

She's scowling at a slouchy middle-aged guy. His hair's as red as mine, but he has dark eyebrows that don't match it. Another government employee? He isn't wearing a uniform. One cheek is covered in freckles. Across the other cheek is a vivid mark, about the size and shape of a human hand. Frieda's hand, I bet. She's strong enough to make a slap really hurt.

I step past Veronica to stare. The policeman from the baggage pickup is in the middle of the room, scratching his head. The dog isn't with him. "What's the trouble?" he asks.

"He wanted me to get out of the wheelchair," says Frieda. "When I said no, he threatened to drag me out."

"Just doing my job, officer," the slouchy guy says in a whiny voice. There's a strong earthy smell in the room. Slouchy wears cologne. "Doing what I'm told, you know? They said to be thorough."

The policeman frowns. "You're supposed to search the chair?"

"I . . . I. . . ." Slouchy looks confused now. He darts a glance at Veronica and me. "I don't know," he says.

"Too bad Lucky's not here," says the policeman. "She's on a kennel break now. Lucky's trained to sniff out contraband. She's a dog," he explains, so we don't think he's talking about another police officer sniffing around. "You wouldn't have to move anyone if Lucky were here. Mind you, if they tell you to look, you have to look. Sorry, miss," he says to Frieda. "But rules are rules. If they say look in the chair, that's what we'll do. Maybe I can help. Where's a good spot to start looking, now? There's pockets here. And plastic caps on the handles. Is the metal hollow? Does the wheelchair come apart, do you know?"

"No, no, no!" The slouchy guy sounds agitated. "It's all right, officer. I've . . . changed my mind. I don't want you to waste your time. Who knows what'll happen if you find something. I've decided there's no need to search the chair. Sorry. You're free to go, Miss Miller."

"You sure?" says the policeman. "You don't want to get in trouble with your boss. Back at the station I'm always getting in trouble with the sarge. She says Lucky has more sense than I do. Ha-ha-ha."

"Ha-ha." The slouchy guy's laugh is not very convincing.

Frieda notices me for the first time. "What are *you* doing?" she says.

And my own problems come back. "My dad's not here," I say. "He's not waiting for me. I have to make a phone call. Veronica," I say, turning to tell her. "I have to phone my dad's work number to find out what happened –"

I stop. Veronica has disappeared.

I step to the door. Can't see her. I run down the corridor. Can't see her. Can't see my dad, either. Frieda wheels herself out of the blue room towards me. The two men follow. The policeman is carrying her suitcase. The slouchy guy puts on a pair of sunglasses and slouches away. His cologne lingers a little uncomfortably, like the last guest to be picked up from your birthday party. Frieda stares after him. The policeman stares at an advertisement for pizza.

I have to phone my dad. There's a bank of pay phones on the wall nearby. I unbutton my pants pocket, reach in and pull out the piece of paper with my dad's office phone number, and the American quarter. I take a step forward. Someone hurries past me, knocking me down. "Sorry," I say, from the ground, but whoever knocked me down is gone. I get up carefully, and find that my American quarter is gone too. I look around for it, but all I see is litter and moving feet.

Uh-oh.

"What am I going to do?" I say loudly. "I need to make a phone call."

"So phone," says Frieda.

"I don't have any money for a phone call. I just lost my only American quarter."

She sighs, and turns away to root around in the purse at her side.

"Huh?" The policeman shakes his head. "You say something about a phone, kid?"

"I have to make a call. I want to talk to my dad," I say.

He listens to me carefully, paying attention to my face. He looks concerned. "Phone call? Sure," he says. "Use my phone."

"Oh, thank you. Thank you."

He reaches into his pocket. Frowns. Reaches into another pocket. "Shoot!" he says. "I must have left it at home. Sorry, kid," he says. "You'll have to find another phone."

"Use mine," says Frieda. From her purse she pulls a genuine cell phone, with an aerial and flashing lights. Just another personal item, like a piece of gum, a tissue, or something. I wonder what else she carries around . . . a ray gun, maybe.

I swallow, stammer my thanks, and punch the number written on the piece of paper. Nothing happens.

"You have to press SEND," she says.

"Sure," I say. I knew that, but I forgot.

The signal is faint. I press the phone against my ear. Now I can make it out. *Ring . . . Ring . . . Ring . . . Ring.* Then a recorded voice cuts in and starts telling me about business hours. "No one's there yet," I say.

I give her back the phone and put the paper back in my pocket. Maybe Dad's just late picking me up. He's often late. Everything could still be okay. I check the crowd again.

No Dad.

"Someone look after me!" That's what I want to say, but I can't. Not in front of Frieda. She may be annoying and bossy, but she sure looks like she's got it all together. This is her city. She's got somewhere to go. She's got someone waiting for her.

Or does she?

She's scanning the crowd. No one's running forward to say welcome home, honey. No one has their arms stretched out to her.

An old lady comes out of the corridor behind us, and is swept up almost at once by a beaming, shouting, hugging mob of people. Frieda and I have to get out of the way.

"Who's coming to pick you up?" I ask.

"No one, I guess," she says. "It was supposed to be Beatrice."

"Your mom?"

"No." She doesn't elaborate.

"Oh. Well, where do you think Beatrice is?"

"Don't know. At home, I guess."

"Where do you think Veronica is?"

"Don't know. It doesn't matter."

"Do you think Beatrice is coming? Do you think Veronica's coming back? What are you going to do?" I say. Of course what I really mean is, what am *I* going to do?

She shrugs. She's not in the least worried.

A cart with shiny mirrored sides rolls by, selling lottery tickets, I think. As it passes us, I catch a glimpse of our reflections. What a contrast! There's Frieda, rich city girl in a neat fitting pantsuit with zips and pockets all over the place. Her arms are tanned and muscular; her hair is sassy and combed. She could be on safari, or on her way to a party, and look fine. As the cart rolls past, she puts the phone back in her purse and pulls out a pair of sunglasses. Perfect.

And there I am in my too-big soccer shirt, with a picture of a donut on the front because the team sponsor is a local donut shop. And shorts with button pockets. My arms and legs are skinny, and where they aren't freckled, they're almost as white as the sunblock Mom makes me wear all summer long. All in all, I look as confident and independent, as together, as a house of cards in a hurricane.

I don't know what to do. I stand and wait for someone to take care of me.

I think about Mom, hiking with the kids she works with. They've got someone to look after them. I think about Dad. Has he really forgotten about me? When I was three, he left me playing under the seats at the ballpark while he went off to buy a hot dog. He was gone for two innings; I thought he'd never come back. To this day I hate peanuts in the shell. Gee, I sound like Mom, reopening old wounds.

"Look, kids, I got a job to do," says the policeman. "I can't baby-sit, you know?" He holds out Frieda's suitcase to me. I take it. "You guys got a place to go?" He thinks we're together, Frieda and I.

"I've got a place to go," says Frieda.

"I don't," I say.

"Oh," says the policeman.

Frieda looks at me, looks away, doesn't say anything.

"Um," says the policeman.

Frieda slides her sunglasses up into her hair, hunts a compact mirror out of her purse, and checks her face. My mom does that too. "I'm going to get a cab," she says.

"Well," says the policeman, rubbing his mustache. "I guess that's okay. The street doors are . . . now, let's see. Which way are they?" He frowns.

"I know the way out," says Frieda.

"Right. Good. Okay, then."

The policeman turns to look at me. I open my mouth. I don't know what I'm going to say, exactly, but I don't think I'm going to be proud of it. Back home in Cobourg I'd been so sure of myself. "Of course I'll be okay," I told my mom. "I'm thirteen," I told her. "I'm independent. I can manage. Don't you worry." Now, I'm the one worrying.

Before any words leave my mouth, Frieda says, "He can come with me."

"Huh?" I say.

"Great!" says the policeman. He's relieved. "That's fine. And if you kids run into trouble, don't hesitate to, um. . . ." He pauses. Neither of us says anything. "Well, you know where I am. Only I'll be off duty soon." He turns, and vanishes back into the corridor.

"Did you mean it?" I say to Frieda. "About me coming with you?"

"Uh-huh."

"You sure?"

"I'm sure," she says, over her shoulder. "Come on, kid, you won't last a minute on your own. Come to my place. You can wait there."

"For the last time, my name's Alan."

"Okay. Alan. Pleased to meet you. Won't you come to my . . . to my *hoos*?" she says, with a snicker. She thinks that's how Canadians say *house*. The way she says it sounds like *howse*.

"Thank you," I say.

"You can hang on to my suitcase," she says, and sets off

into the crowd. I take one last look for my father, then follow, laboring.

Actually, there isn't much labor. I carry my soccer bag over my shoulder, and her suitcase in my hand. Before Frieda has arm-pushed three times and I've taken twenty steps, we're on a moving sidewalk. A perfect vehicle for the big city; you can go fast even when you're standing still. I put down the bags and rest.

"So, who's Beatrice?" I ask. None of my business, I just want to make conversation. "An aunt or something?"

"She's my nanny."

"Oh." I've never met a kid with a nanny. I started to read a book about one once. The kid was so polite and nice, I wanted to punch him. You know what they say on book covers: *I couldn't put it down!* Well, I could put that book down all right. And I did.

"Do you want to phone your nanny?" I say.

"No," she says.

The voice that comes over the loudspeakers in airports and train stations – the voice no one can understand, even if it's speaking in their own language – tells us about an incoming flight from . . . home, I think. *Home* is what I hear. Unless it's *Nome*. Nome is in Alaska, isn't it? I'm a long way from Nome. Home, too.

This section of moving sidewalk ends. Two other sidewalks go off from it in two different directions. There's a sign beside one of them: CLOSED TO PUBLIC – MOVIE EXTRAS THIS WAY. A man with uncombed hair stands beside the sign. His eyes are closed. He's got a headset and a clipboard. He slurps coffee from a Styrofoam cup.

"Hey, they're shooting a movie," I say to Frieda.

"Yeah, so?" she says.

"Right here in the airport. Cool."

"Cool? You say that, where you come from? Cool?"

"I wonder who's in the movie?"

"I don't care."

No one else seems to care either. I guess New York is used to movies. I'm not. They shot a made-for-TV movie in Cobourg a few years ago, and we're still talking about it. My mom and her girlfriends spent an entire weekend walking up and down in front of the set, hoping to get a glimpse of a star who used to model underwear.

"Watch it, kid!"

Frieda reaches to push me – hard. Clutching our bags, I stumble out of the way of a motorized cart full of other people's luggage. The stickers on the bags say LEONARDO DA VINCI AEROGARDE, ROMA, ITALIA. Rome, I guess. Probably what the loudspeaker voice was saying. Not *Home*, or *Nome*.

"Thanks," I say to Frieda, who doesn't reply. I follow her onto the next section of moving sidewalk. The sign up ahead says WAY OUT – BUSES AND TAXIS. The sidewalk is moving us quickly towards it, as if it wants us to go this way.

Frieda's staring at something up ahead on the left. "Hey!" she says in a whisper. "Hey, Alan, look over there, behind the pillar. Who do you see?"

I turn, and peer closely. "No one," I say.

"I thought I saw the guy with the dyed red hair and the cologne – you know, the guy I slapped," she says.

"Oh." I stare, backwards now, because we're still moving. "I don't see him," I say.

"He was pretty creepy, wasn't he? And the other guy – the skinny government guy – acted funny too."

"Do you really think that red hair was dyed?" I ask.

She frowns up at me. "With those dark eyebrows? Of course."

"He's not that old. I thought only old guys dyed their hair."

"This sounds crazy, Alan, but I think he was after . . . me. He was interested in me. So was the skinny guy."

"He was interested in your Horus the dentist earrings," I say.

She doesn't smile. "There's a lot of kidnapping going on these days," she says. "We get taught about it in school. How to avoid it."

An amazing idea. What kind of school does she go to, I wonder? "We get taught about fire safety," I say. "And to look both ways before crossing the street."

"I wonder if they want to kidnap me."

Is she kidding? She's got to be kidding. Kidnapping is like floods and earthquakes and civil war. It happens far away, to strangers.

"One of my classmates got kidnapped last year, you know. Her parents had to pay a hundred thousand dollars to get her back."

She's not kidding. I choke. Bad enough to be on my own in New York City. Now I'm thinking about being on my own with kidnappers.

"Let's go back," I say. "We'll go back to the policeman."

"No."

"Yes." There's a sidewalk moving the other way. It'd be easy enough to hop across. I turn my head to see if anyone's coming – looking both ways, like they teach us in school – and there he is! He's well back of us, behind a bunch of people, but he's on our moving sidewalk. I know it's him. He sees me looking, and immediately ducks his dyed red head, as if he doesn't want me to notice him.

3

It's Not My Dog!

"Oh, no! He's behind us!" I whisper. Not that he could hear me.

"Who? The slouchy guy, with the dyed hair? You saw him?"

"What'll we do? What'll we do?" I look around for a police officer. There isn't one. "Help!" I call, to . . . well, I don't know who. I look up, maybe for a sign from the heavens, but we're still inside.

"First, we'll get a cab," says Frieda.

She pushes off. The wheelchair skitters forward on the moving sidewalk. I follow her as fast as I can. People get out of our way.

"Do you have enough money?" I ask breathlessly.

"I have a fifty-dollar bill in my purse," says Frieda. "My dad says you should never travel without a fifty-dollar bill for emergencies."

An amazing idea. What kind of parents does she have?
"My mom says you should never run with scissors," I say.

The moving sidewalk ends. The doors to the outside open automatically. There's a crowd of people waiting for a line of yellow taxis. It's a lovely clear morning, now, but a gang of dark clouds are chasing the sun across the sky. Sooner or later they're going to catch it.

There's a problem with the cab at the head of the line. An old lady is complaining, pointing with her cane at the cab. The cabdriver is trying to explain something.

"I tell you, it's not my dog," he says. "She just hangs around here. Ask anyone! Ask Harvey, there. Hey, Harvey, is this my dog?"

Harvey is a big fat man in a tight shirt. He clambers out of his cab, the next in line.

"That's Sally," he says.

"Is she my dog?"

"Nope. She's no one's dog. She just hangs around here. She likes to take cab rides."

"You see?" says the first cabdriver. He opens the door to his cab, and a dog climbs out.

Funny-looking dog – about the size of a police dog, but with huge pointy ears, like a bat. The ears stick straight up, and give the dog a permanently surprised expression.

"Oh, the sweetie!" says Frieda.

The old lady stamps on the ground with her cane. "But the . . . the *animal* has been inside the cab. I will not ride in a cab where an animal has been!"

A man with a briefcase and cigar brushes past her. "I'll ride with anything," he says, getting into the first cab. "Borough courthouse," he directs the driver. "And step on it."

The first cab drives off. Harvey gets back in his cab. The whole line of cabs moves forward. The old lady opens the door to Harvey's cab. And Sally the dog climbs in.

I look behind me. I don't see Slouchy. People are milling around, complaining about the old lady, the delay, the humidity. I take a deep breath, and, oddly enough, feel myself carried away, out of the present. For a moment it's as if nothing has gone wrong yet. I feel hopeful: my dad *is* waiting for me; we'll shake hands and go to the hotel, where there'll be a swimming pool and a video game player, and we'll order room service, and I'll get to stay up late.

False hope.

"Hi, there."

I'm back to reality – back to panic. It's Slouchy. He's caught up to us. He's wearing a windbreaker and sunglasses. He slouches up to Frieda, smiling. One of his teeth is silver. It glints. "Here we are again," he says.

Frieda doesn't answer. She rolls herself over to me for moral support. I hope she doesn't want any other kind. Slouchy smiles at me too. And takes a candy bar from his pocket.

"What a coincidence," he says. "I'm just off work and you're waiting for a lift. It's . . . Frieda, right? Frieda Miller? I remember the name from your suitcase."

He smiles and unwraps the candy bar. She's right. He *is* creepy.

"Want a bite?" he asks. "I've got more in my pocket. This one's caramel."

"No," says Frieda.

"I hope you don't think I'm sore about that slap you gave me," he says. "The mark's gone, and I've totally forgotten about it. A misunderstanding. Friends, okay?"

Frieda doesn't say anything.

"Say!" he exclaims, as if he's just got the idea. "How about coming with me? I've got a car waiting. Me and my cousin would be happy to give you a ride home."

"That's okay," she says. "We can take a cab."

"Oh, but taxis are so expensive. And the drivers don't always know where you want to go. Better come with us."

"No," says Frieda.

"We'll save you taxi fare. Your parents will appreciate it. They'll love you for saving them money – mark my words."

"They will? *My* parents?" Frieda laughs – not happily. "You don't know them," she says.

Slouchy raises his hand and beckons. A blue car I haven't noticed pulls up to the front of the cab rank. It looks like a whole lot of other cars, except for the pink tassel tied to the aerial.

Slouchy opens the back door for us. "Come on," he says. "You'll be home in no time."

The driver is the skinny government employee with the long nose and the federal powers. "Plenty of room," he rasps.

All this time the taxis have been sliding forward, one at a time, like pop cans in a vending machine. The funny-looking dog, Sally, is frisking up and down the line, jumping in and out of the waiting cabs. The crabby old lady is tired and upset. Poor crabby old lady.

Skinny's car is ahead of all the cabs. Sally chases the old lady towards it. When she gets to the open door, she practically collapses onto Skinny's backseat. "Thank you, thank you," she says to Slouchy, who stares at her, openmouthed, his silver tooth gleaming. "I live at the Northwestern Hotel, in Manhattan," she says, mistaking Skinny for a taxi driver. "No pets allowed." She reaches out, and closes the car door firmly in Sally's face.

Sally backs into Frieda's wheelchair, and stands there, quivering. Frieda reaches out and strokes her flank.

Slouchy scowls at the old lady. Puts his hand on the door. Then he takes a sudden step back, and starts shaking his head. He waves his arms around, slapping at his neck irritably. "Bees," he says. "I hate bees."

I look up – now I'm outside, I can see the sky – but I still don't see any sign from heaven. Or do I? There seems to be a flash of something small and golden hovering near Slouchy's neck. . . .

Sally's big bat ears twitch. She runs over to Slouchy and starts barking and leaping up. She wants the candy bar. She's a big dog. Big enough to put her paws on Slouchy's chest when she jumps. He stumbles backwards, along the length of the car. Sally's jaws snap together, near the candy bar. Near the bee too.

– *Watch out!*

The voice is high-pitched. Not Slouchy's voice. He uses the front door handle to pull himself to his feet. He's staring around like a man who's heard a ghost. Sally jumps again, knocking him down.

– *Beat it! Go away!*

The voice again. Can it be? I'm sure I know the voice well. "Norbert?" I say, taking a step forward. "Is that you?"

Sally, very excited, jumps again. The candy bar, and the bee, disappear.

Slouchy is lying on his back beside the car. "All right, all right," he mutters to himself. "I'll beat it." He fumbles the car door open and crawls in. Skinny drives away. And, echoing strangely, the voice returns once more.

– *Great steaming mugs of cocoa! Where am I?*

The dog stands perfectly still for a moment. Then she sneezes three times in a row. Then she circles herself, chasing her tail. Then she sneezes once more, very loudly, and sits down. The expression on her face reminds me of the time my friend Victor ate what he thought was a jelly-bean, only it turned out to be a bath oil bead.

The cab line moves forward. People get in. Cabs drive off. Nobody's paying attention to us. Sally moves over to Frieda's wheelchair and puts her paws up on Frieda's lap. Frieda strokes the dog's head, tentatively.

"Hi, there, sweetie," she says.

Sally makes a snuffling sound.

"Aren't you beautiful," says Frieda.

– *Thank you, I suppose I am.*

"Norbert," I say. "So it really *is* you." I know it's Norbert. It's his voice, and it's just the kind of thing he'd say.

Frieda gives a little shriek, and draws back. But she doesn't let go of the dog.

"Is that you talking, Alan?" she says. "Or is it the dog?"

"Neither one of us, actually," I say.

I try to explain it to her. Norbert is a tiny, squeaky-voiced alien from the planet Jupiter. For a while last year he lived inside my nose, the way a friend would stay over at your place while his parents are out of town. Norbert didn't feel cramped. Apparently my nose is bigger than I thought, with a living room inside. Yes, I said *living room.* There's also a bedroom, a back room, a kitchen, and a garage for Norbert's spaceship.

No, I don't understand it either. Norbert stayed with me for a few weeks, and then left to live in k.d. lang's nose. Yes, the singer k.d. lang. Apparently the whole planet Jupiter just loves our country music. As far as I know, Norbert's been with Ms. lang ever since.

I've kind of missed him.

– *Yes, it's really me,* he says, from down beside my knee. *You called for help, didn't you? Who were you expecting – Mighty Mouse?*

I should say that Norbert is not always polite. In fact, he's quite a mouthy little fellow.

"Where are you? Are you . . . inside the dog?"

Sally barks.

"Inside the dog's . . . nose?"

– *Hey, it's a lot roomier than yours, Dingwall. It was a shock at first, landing in here, but I've had a chance to look round, now, and I think I like it. I've got a studio, you know, with two skylights. I may take up oil painting again.*

Frieda frowns at Sally. "You can talk," she whispers.

– *Yes, I can. So can you. So can Dingwall, here, which means it can't be that tough.*

"Hey!" I say.

– *See what I mean?* says Norbert. *A blushing Demosthenes.*

Of course I am blushing. Frieda smiles slightly. "But you're talking to . . . to me," she says.

– *Oh my achy breaky heart! Come on, girlie! Try to catch up. I am speaking to you. You are speaking to me. It's called conversation.*

Can the people nearby hear? No one turns around. No one notices.

"Norbert! That's rude!" I say.

Funny, I wouldn't have cared what anyone said to Frieda on the plane. She is, after all, an annoying girl. I figure it's her wheelchair that makes me want her treated more nicely. Being in a wheelchair makes her more vulnerable. Why is it, I wonder, that you only want to be polite to someone because they're already in trouble? After all, she's still an annoying girl.

The dog looks up at Frieda, and barks. Frieda's expression clears. She strokes the dog.

– *Shut up, Sally,* says Norbert. *Quick now, Dingwall. Where are we going?*

4

Not Uncool

"We?" I say. "You mean, you're coming with us?"

– *Of course.*

I can't tell you what a weight that is off my back. Norbert is difficult at times, rude and opinionated, but he's on my side. He's a friend. And he doesn't get scared. Not ever. It's a real asset to have a friend who's never afraid.

– *D'you want help or not? You asked for it. And, in my opinion, you need all the help you can get. Who picked your clothes for you? And when did you start wearing cologne? You smell like last week's roses.*

Frieda giggles.

I can feel myself blushing again. "That's not my cologne," I say.

– *This young lady here is dressed very nicely indeed. k.d. lang has a suit almost exactly like it. And you, Dingwall, are wearing a shirt with a donut on it. Now, where are we going?*

Frieda stops giggling to say, "My place. My parents' place."

"My dad was supposed to meet me," I say. "But he's not here."

The line of cabs moves forward again. The driver in front slams on his brakes, forcing the other cabs to stop suddenly too.

– *Hey, TAXI!* yells Norbert. Frieda stares at him – well, at Sally.

A businessman with a fat briefcase is moving past us, gesturing at the cab.

– *Back off, buster,* snarls Norbert. *That's our cab.*

The man turns around with a frown. "Didn't anyone teach you manners, young lady?" he says. The dog's head is near Frieda's. The businessman figures Frieda is talking.

– *Manners? You're a cab thief, and you talk about manners! I'd have this mutt bite you in the leg, if I could get her to do what she's told.*

Norbert is mad.

– *Hey, Dingwall. The girlie isn't moving. Push her. Make with the feet, big guy!*

The cabdriver is trying to find the switch that opens the trunk. He opens the hood by mistake, and turns on the windshield wipers. I help Frieda out of the chair and into the cab. She leans on me. Finally the cabdriver figures out how to open the trunk. The wheelchair fits inside after I fold it up. Sally jumps into the cab after Frieda. I climb in last. It's a tight fit.

The businessman is staring at us.

– *And your shoelace is untied!* Norbert shouts past my shoulder. The businessman looks down. A man and a woman, holding hands, push past him. He drops his briefcase. It opens. Papers fly out. Norbert's laugh sounds funny coming from a dog.

"Where to?" asks the driver.

"Take us to 26 West 84th Street," says Frieda, loud and clear. "It's off Central Park West. In Manhattan," she adds.

"Show me some money," says the driver.

Frieda's purse is on her shoulder now. She reaches in and finds a bill. Holds it up.

The driver pulls down the flag to start the meter, and takes off like a rocket.

No one says anything at first. The cabdriver concentrates on the traffic, muttering to himself. I stare out the window.

A few minutes later I hear Frieda's voice. She's not talking to me.

– *Pleased to meet you too, Frieda,* Norbert replies. *Pardon my earlier rudeness. Excuse me while I wipe my cocoa mustache. On Jupiter we all drink cocoa. Now I have to clean up the dishes. I must say, Sally's kitchen has every modern convenience.*

We have to stop at a traffic light. The cabdriver shakes his head. When the light turns green, he takes off with a squeal of tires.

"So your dad is a state representative," I say. "That's important, isn't it?"

Frieda stares. "Of course it is. Don't you know anything? Don't they have state representatives where you come from?"

"I'm from Canada," I say. "We don't even have states."

She shakes her head. "Not unweird," she says.

– *k.d. lang's favorite place in the world is a little town in Alberta, Canada,* says Norbert.

"But Alberta is a state," says Frieda. "Right above North Dakota."

"It is?" I say. It's my country, but she sounds so darn sure of herself, I think maybe I've missed something in the news. "Are you sure?"

"Of course I'm sure. My dad went there last year and he's a politician."

"Do you think that's why they're after you?" I ask. "Because of politics? Because of your dad?"

Frieda shrugs her shoulders. "Maybe," she says. "What does your dad do?"

"He works in human resources," I say. "He keeps getting transferred. This is his first year in New York. My mom helps children in trouble. What does your mom do?"

Her face shuts tight, like a slammed door. "Nothing," she says.

We're driving across a bridge I've seen a million times before, on TV and at the movies. I recognize the view ahead of me, with the morning sun shining on all the famous skyscrapers.

"Cool," I say. I can't help it. I know it's scary and all, and I'm in a strange city, and my dad is too busy to pick up his son at the airport, but it is pretty cool. Only I'm wrong.

"In New York, nothing is cool," says Frieda.

"Sure it is," I say. "This is cool."

"'Cool' is just not a cool expression," she explains. "That is, what you would call cool."

I have to believe her. She's so certain. "When something is cool, what do you call it?"

She smiles. "We call it: not uncool."

"Not uncool!" I try it out. "Sounds dumb."

"And 'cool' sounds smart?"

I don't have anything to say to that.

– *On Jupiter,* says Norbert, *we say that something is very "Sid."*

"'Sid?'" says Frieda.

– *Yes, Sid. Like the moon. One of Jupiter's moons is named Sid.*

"I didn't know that," she says.

Frieda seems to have adjusted to Norbert. Maybe because she's from the city. There're already so many different kinds of people in a place like New York that one more stranger – no matter how strange – is easier to accept. I tried to tell people about Norbert last year, but no one would believe me. They thought it was me talking.

"So, Norbert, what do you think of the Queensboro Bridge?" she says. "Is it Sid?"

– *Well, it's not unSid.*

"Not bad for you!" she says, stroking the dog's ears. Sally tosses her head. We laugh. Seems like the first time in weeks that I've laughed.

Finally I start to relax. This whole adventure may well be over soon. Dad'll pick me up from Frieda's place, and we'll drive to the hotel, and unpack my . . .

"Oh, no!" I say.

Frieda is turned around in her seat, so she can look out the back window.

"Our luggage. We don't have our bags." In the hurry of getting away from the airport, I forgot about them. Her suitcase and my soccer bag are on the sidewalk in front of the cab rank. "We'll have to go back and get them," I say.

Frieda keeps staring back, as if she doesn't care at all about the luggage. I can't understand why, until I realize that the car she's staring at, the car directly behind us, has a pink tassel tied to the aerial.

We're being followed by Slouchy and Skinny. And maybe the crabby old lady, but I'm not too worried about her.

I don't care about the luggage either. This is much more important. I thought all the bad stuff was over. I feel like crying. I don't know what to do. Fortunately, Norbert is decisive.

– *We must find a way to lose the car. k.d. lang's driver used to turn three times really fast to discourage pepperonis.*

"Pepperonis?" I say.

– *I think she said "pepperonis." I hope our driver is as good as Mario. Hey, up front! Hey, there!*

The cabdriver frowns, turns right around so that one arm is along the front seat. The car sails across a lane of traffic. "You talking to me?" he says. His eyes dance in his head.

– *Yes,* says Norbert.

"Are you," he pauses, staring at the dog, "talking to me?"

– *Yes. Are you listening?*

"Me?" he says. "You're talking to me?"

The bridge is behind us on our left. Buildings tower over us. The cab swoops across the road. As we approach the next intersection, the driver turns around even farther to stare at us. This movement puts the wheel down. I shut my eyes. When I open them again, we're on a different street, with the sun behind us. Somehow, we made the turn.

We haven't hit anyone yet, partly because we are incredibly lucky, and partly because New York drivers seem to be very alert to odd behavior on the part of other drivers.

– *Yes,* says Norbert. *Yes, I'm talking to you.* Dog and driver stare at each other. We're driving down a one-way street, but the arrow is pointing towards us. We're going the wrong way. Fortunately, no one else is on the street. The driver shakes his head, causing the cab to make another unexpected turn down another street. I breathe a sigh of relief. I have no idea where we're headed, but at least we're going in the same direction as everyone else.

– *What part of "yes" don't you understand?* Norbert asks.

The driver shudders all over, then turns back around, grabbing the steering wheel just in time to avoid a truck in the lane next to ours. "That's it," he says, in his grating voice. "Talking spiders, talking toilets. Now talking dogs. I've got to get away." He speeds up.

I look around for the car with the pink tassel, but I can't find it. I guess the skinny government man can't keep up with our driver's traffic antics. That's one piece of good news.

Frieda's giggling. She seems a lot younger when she giggles.

"What's funny?" I ask her.

"Talking toilets," she sputters.

The cabdriver pulls over suddenly, the way he does everything else. "Where's my money?" he says.

Frieda stops giggling. She peers out the window. "Wait a minute," she says. She still has the bill in her hand.

The cabdriver reaches back and takes it.

"But we're not home," she says. "This is Rockefeller Center. We're way too far downtown."

The driver ignores her. He points a forefinger at Sally. "We'll meet again," he says.

– *Not if I can help it.*

The driver gets out of the car.

"Hey, my change!" cries Frieda. "Stop, thief! Stop him, Alan!"

I unroll the window. "Hey, Émile!" That's the name on the cab licence displayed on the back of the front seat. Émile Rodomar. He walks past a tall thin tower. He doesn't look back. The meter ticks on.

"Great job of stopping him," Frieda says. "What are we going to do now? I don't have any more money." She checks her purse. "A dollar bill, three quarters, a dime, and some pennies. That's about enough to buy a glass of water."

Sally barks. Frieda pats her absently. "Hey, look here. It's not even him." Frieda points to the picture of Émile on the cab licence – it doesn't look anything like our driver.

"We're in a stolen cab," says Frieda.

Sally keeps barking.

– *She wants out,* says Norbert.

"Why?" I ask.

– *Just let her out.*

"Oh."

I open the door for the dog, get out myself, then reach back in to help Frieda. She pushes my hand away. I stand on the sidewalk and watch as she levers herself out of the cab with her arms, and leans awkwardly against the door.

An elderly man almost knocks me over. "Sorry," I say to him, but he's already out of earshot. The whole city seems to be in a hurry. Pedestrians whiz by like racing cars. Traffic whizzes by at the speed of light. And, on the subject of whizzing. . . .

"Norbert?" I look around for him. "Where did you – oh, there you are." Sally comes frisking up, her tail wagging, her big ears cocked alertly.

"Don't just stand there," Frieda says to me. "If you want to help, get my chair out of the trunk. I hope you like walking. It's going to take us hours to get to my place from here."

"Walking?" I say.

"Good thing you left the luggage behind," she says.

"Can't we phone someone," I say, "or take a cab?"

"What's the matter? Embarrassed?"

"Why?" I blush easily. It's the only thing I have in common with my dad. "Why should I be embarrassed?"

I pop the trunk and fetch her wheelchair. She won't let me help her into it.

"I could phone home, I suppose, but no one will answer. And with $1.96, we sure aren't taking any cabs."

"Let me phone," I say. She hands me the phone without a word.

I dial from memory. Someone picks up after only one ring. "Hello? Who wants pizza?"

"Dad?"

There's a long pause. "I sure hope not," he says.

"Dad, it's me, Alan."

"Who? Talk louder. I can't hear you."

I tell him my name again.

"Who gave you that name? Alan? What kind of name is *Alan*? Sounds like a violin player's name. You play the violin, Alan?" Is he making a joke? It doesn't sound like his voice, exactly. He pronounces my name *Yell-an*. Is Dad pretending to have a New York accent?

"You know I don't, Dad."

"I don't know anything about you," he says. "Except your name, which I don't like. Listen, you want a pizza or don't you?"

"Pizza?"

"You dial Mike's Pizza, you want pizza. Am I right? Course I'm right."

"I want my father," I say.

"Then try the adoption agency. And while you're there, see if they'll give you a new name. Ask for something a bit spicier. Jake, maybe. That's a good name." His voice is growing really faint now. "And put down the violin."

I hold the phone away from my ear.

"Wrong number?" asks Frieda.

"I hope so," I say.

I get out my piece of paper and punch the correct numbers. And SEND.

My dad says hello. His voice sounds far away and faint, but it's *his* voice. I almost cry.

"Dad! Am I ever glad to –"

He interrupts me to say that it's Monday, July 10th, and he is away from his desk right now. If I care to leave a message, I can do so at the sound of the tone. I wait and wait, but there's no tone. I can't tell if he's hung up. "Hello? Hello?"

"Well?" Frieda says.

"I don't know." I hand her the phone.

"There's the problem." She points to a flickering signal light. "Out of power."

"What do you mean?"

"The phone needs recharging. I meant to do it in Toronto, but I forgot."

I grab the phone from her hands and try the number again. I can't hear anything.

"What now?" I say. "Are we really going to walk all the way to your place?"

She smiles bitterly. "*You're* going to walk," she says.

5

My World Is Bigger

– So there we were on the couch, talking to the doctor. k.d. lang was lying down. I was in a chair in the front room with a mug of cocoa. The doctor was very curious about me, kept wanting to know more about my childhood on Jupiter. And when I finally ran out of gossip, the doctor said, "Ms. lang, I really think you should go ahead with the procedure."

We've walked a few blocks along 50th Street, and now we're walking up Broadway. All right, Sally and I are walking. Frieda is rolling. It's up because the numbers of the cross streets are getting bigger. 50 . . . 51. Norbert is explaining how he got here to New York from Los Angeles, where k.d. lang was staying.

– "But I like my nose," she told the doctor. "I don't want to look like someone else." "Good for you," I said. And the doctor frowned, and made a note.

"You were talking to a therapist," says Frieda. She's leading the way. She turns her head to face Sally. "Weren't you?"

– A therapist, that's right. k.d. got the name from a friend, shortly after I arrived.

I laugh. "A therapist? Like a crazy doctor? A shrink? Poor k.d. lang."

"I see a therapist sometimes," says Frieda.

"Oh." Smart, Dingwall. Very smart. "Sorry," I say.

We come to an intersection. The light turns yellow. The DON'T WALK sign appears. I slow down, but Frieda keeps going. I reach out to grab the wheelchair so that she can stop in plenty of time. "What are you doing?" she snaps over her shoulder. No one else stops. In fact, they speed up. A man runs into us from behind, bangs his knee pretty good, and hobbles out onto the street anyway. A lady hurries past us. "What's with you?" she says. A car turns the corner, just missing the hobbling man. The car behind it just misses the hurrying lady. The light changes from yellow to red. Horns blow. Traffic shoots ahead, as if from a catapult.

"Hayseed!" says Frieda. "In New York, you have to move fast."

"I can move faster than you!" Of course it's a bad thing to say, but when I'm talking to Frieda I keep forgetting she's in a wheelchair. The light is still red for us. Sally is sniffing something on the sidewalk, which upsets Norbert.

– Leave it alone! It's dirty. You don't know what that is, Sally. What do you mean, you do know what that is? What is it? Oh, great galaxies, NO! Come on, Sally. How many times do I have to tell you. . . .

Poor Norbert. The light turns green. The WALK sign appears. We move forward. A car turns the corner, slams on its brakes, just missing us. Frieda ignores it.

"But Norbert, what procedure was k.d. lang's therapist talking about?" she asks.

– I didn't understand it either, at first. I tried to ask, but the doctor wouldn't answer my questions. "You can control your own nose, Ms. lang," she said. "You don't have to listen to it. I think a simple rhinoplasty – even if it doesn't change the shape – would be very therapeutic."

Frieda laughs. "They were talking about a nose job, weren't they?"

– I gave them a piece of my mind, I can tell you. I packed last night, and left this morning. Poor Nerissa was upset when I told her. She's a big fan.

"Who's Nerissa?" asks Frieda.

"A . . . friend," I explain. "Back home on Jupiter." I think she's more than just a friend, but I don't feel like getting into that with Frieda.

"Can you talk to Jupiter by telephone, Norbert?"

– Well, it's a long distance call.

No one says anything for a moment.

– She asked for help, you know.

"Who?" asks Frieda. "k.d. lang?"

– That's why I went to L.A. Do you know what it's like to realize you're not wanted?

Frieda doesn't say anything. Her face is shut again.

New York is full of people who live and work on the street. Homeless people, of course, in boxes and doorways. Any big city has them. But New York streets offer more possibilities than most. I see people selling and eating stuff I've never seen before. I don't even recognize the writing on the side of the carts. We pass a woman whose office is on the sidewalk. There's a desk, a lamp, a wastebasket, a chair for clients, and a sign offering advice about income tax. Further along, a well-dressed man promises to find you an acceptable parking solution. I didn't realize there was a parking problem, but Frieda assures me there is.

It starts to rain when we get up to 55th Street. I cross – quickly – and duck under an awning with Frieda. Sally runs in circles around us.

"Buy an umbrella?" asks a pimply teenager. Where'd he come from? He wasn't here a second ago, when it was sunny. Now it's raining and his arms are full of umbrellas. There's another umbrella guy across the street. It's like they spring from the pavement fully equipped, like the soldiers who grow from dragon's teeth in the Greek myth.

"No, thanks," says Frieda.

I wonder how the lady with the desk outside handles the rain.

The store in front of us sells men's clothing. I stare at the suit in the window. Could that price be right? It looks like what you'd pay to buy the building. And speaking of buildings, across the street and down a bit from the umbrella salesman is the coolest – sorry, I'm going to have to work at this – the most not uncool building I've ever seen: soaring, rounded, rippled, as if the wind were the architect. A great combination of the futuristic and the familiar – like a cross between a missile and a thermos. I ask Frieda what building it is. She shrugs.

"I don't know," she says. "Insurance, maybe. Or Public Utilities."

Public Utilities? A boring idea for such a great building. There's a Public Utilities building in Cobourg, right next to the Toronto Dominion bank. My teacher's sister works there.

Suddenly, I want to talk to someone from home. Mom will be out hiking. I could phone Miranda, I suppose. Or Victor. Except, what would I tell him? "Hi, Vic. I'm somewhere in New York City with no money and nowhere to go. Oh, yes, and a couple of bad guys are after me."

Drat Dad anyway. And drat Slouchy and his dyed hair and Skinny and his federal powers, and Veronica, and Frieda. Drat them all.

The rain has stopped. The umbrella salesmen have all vanished. We push on.

Broadway is, well, broad. Looking up, I can see a big strip of gray sky. I have no idea where the sun is – somewhere behind the tall building on our right, I think. We pass a wide entrance, with steps going down. Hot stale air hits my nostrils. A rattle and hum of the trains underfoot. Subway. I think about Frieda getting down the steps. I don't see how she can do it by herself. I don't see how I can help her. She hasn't mentioned taking the subway.

Coming towards us, working his arms like a windmill, is a man in a wheelchair. Shaved head, sunglasses, black chin beard, he looks tough but nice. In a movie he'd be the bad guy who saves the little boy's life just before going to jail.

"How you all doing?" he says, with a special smile for Frieda.

"Fine," I say, trying not to stare.

"Great day," he says, disappearing quickly into the crowd behind us.

Frieda sinks lower in her chair after he's gone. She thrusts herself forward sharply, knocking her hand against the spokes. She's done it before; her knuckles are bruised. She jerks her hand away from the wheel, and there's a tearing sound. She swears.

"You okay?" I ask her.

"My suit isn't." She holds up her arm.

"I don't see anything."

"See?" She shows me a tiny rip on the inside of the right sleeve. She must have caught it on the chair. "See that?"

"That's okay. You can hardly notice it," I say.

"Shut up," she tells me. So I do.

The light ahead turns yellow. I know to speed up now. All around us people are striding faster, making sure they get through the intersection before the traffic starts moving the other way.

I can't help thinking of Cobourg, where cars actually wait on a green light so that oncoming traffic can make a left turn.

On the other side of the intersection, still moving fast, we almost run into an elderly couple in matching orange track-suits. For a moment I actually feel angry at them. What are they doing in my way? Sidewalk rage. Fortunately, it doesn't last long. "Sorry," I tell them, hurrying on.

Frieda hears me. "Don't say sorry," she says. "It shows you're from out of town."

"Sorry," I tell her.

I caught my first fish when I was six years old. It was pretty small: I could have mounted it on a postcard. To be honest, I didn't even catch it. I reeled in my line after sitting for hours in the boat, picking at my peeling sunburn, and found a small dead perch on my hook. My uncle figured it had died of boredom. But I was only six years old, and proud of myself. I carried the poor dead thing around all afternoon, showing it off to neighbors and relatives. And – this is my point – all that week I saw people with fishing rods and tackle boxes. I'm sure they'd been there all along. But I didn't notice them until I caught my fish. Of course I nodded to them, knowingly, as if to say, me too! Experience had broadened my world to include people who had, until then, been invisible to me.

Now I realize I have never seen so many people in wheelchairs. I'm sure they've been here all along, like the guys carrying fishing rods. But because I'm with Frieda, I seem to see wheelchairs everywhere. My attention is caught by a young man in a motorized chair. His body's spiraled up in spasm. His head's on one side. His hands are twisted claws. He's doing fine. On the side of his chair are five people-shaped stencils. Underneath is the legend: DRIVING ACE.

The wheelchair community, like the fishers', is very welcoming to other members. They all have a smile for Frieda. They even smile at me, because I'm with her. The driving ace waves as he passes. "Hi, guys!" he shouts. Not uncool. My world is bigger.

We come to a phone booth. Not a booth, really, just a phone on a pole. "I could call my dad from here," I say. "Got a quarter?"

"Not here," says Frieda.

"Why? You could call too. Maybe someone can come and get us," I say.

"Not here," says Frieda again.

"But why?"

"Because the phone is broken."

She can't even see it. I go closer. The phone *is* broken. How did she know?

There's a small hunched-over lady in a wheelchair waiting by a bus stop with a bunch of nondisabled people. Sounds funny to call them that. *Us*, I suppose I should say. I don't know what the hunched-over lady is waiting for. If she can't get down the steps to the subway, no way can she get up the steps into the bus.

A businessman goes past, talking into his cell phone. I'd like to borrow his phone, but I'm too shy to interrupt.

Another block, and we come to the biggest intersection I've ever seen. It's a circle with two wide roads cutting through the center of it, and then splitting off in five or six directions, like spokes from the hub of a wheel. Part of the circle leads to a park, a real park with grass.

We cross three streets. I follow Frieda. When we get to the park, she calls a halt.

"Good idea," I tell her. "I'm feeling a bit tired."

"We're not stopping for you," she says. "It's for Sally."

I look round. Sally's right here, the way she always is. An obedient dog. Her tongue is lolling a bit, and she looks tired. When she hears her name, she comes over to the wheelchair and puts her head in Frieda's lap.

"What's wrong with her?" I ask.

"She's thirsty," says Frieda. "Look at her, panting, the poor thing."

The only living creature that Frieda speaks kindly to. I wonder if the dog appreciates it.

– *There's no cold water in the kitchen tap,* says Norbert. *Only hot, and not much of that.*

"You see," says Frieda. "Why don't you give her a drink."

There's a water fountain nearby – a square stone pillar about chest height, with a push button on the side. No one's using it.

"How am I going to give her a drink?" I say. I look around for a dish, or something to put the water into. Nothing. I turn on the fountain. Sally gives a little yelp and hurries over. She stands on her hind legs and reaches up with her paws, but she can't quite reach. She'd look funny if she weren't so eager, so desperate.

I catch sight of Frieda, whose face mirrors the dog's distress. It occurs to me that Frieda might be as thirsty as

Sally. She probably can't reach the fountain either. No, that can't be right; I've seen Frieda stand up for a moment before getting into the cab. But I'll bet she knows what it's like to be unable to do something, through no fault of your own.

Sally looks for help – not to me, standing next to her with my thumb on the fountain button, but to Frieda.

Frieda rolls herself over. Sally scrambles, with difficulty, onto Frieda's lap. She's a big dog. She can reach the water easily now. Her paws go right over the fountain. Frieda holds her from behind. The chair starts to roll backwards. When I grab for the chair, I let go of the button. The spray of water disappears. Sally whines and laps frantically.

"Lock the chair," Frieda says, from behind a mouthful of dog fur.

I fumble around helplessly.

"There's a brake pedal at the back. Push it down," she says.

I keep fumbling.

"And turn the water back on."

I'm down on my knees. I lock the wheelchair, reach up and turn on the fountain. Water hits Sally in the muzzle and sprays everywhere. Including on me. I hear laughter. I scramble to my feet. Sally's going crazy. Frieda is hanging on grimly.

The laughter comes from a group of little kids standing nearby. They keep laughing as Sally drinks. They're holding hands; and they all have bright yellow hats. A day care. A woman with a matching hat – and doesn't she look tired! – counts heads every few seconds. Half of the kids have sunglasses, even though the day has turned cloudy.

Sally finishes drinking, shakes her head, and leaps off Frieda's lap. I take the brake off Frieda's chair. She rolls herself away. The kids applaud. The tired lady starts shepherding them into line beside the fountain.

An old man in Bermuda shorts shuffles past. He looks like a tortoise – slow, wrinkly, and disapproving. The velcro flap on one of his walking shoes is loose. "Disgusting!" His lipless mouth snaps shut on the word, then opens again. "Absolutely disgusting!" He bends down to pull the velcro tight. The ring on his finger catches my eye. Big and gold. "People use that drinking fountain," he says.

He's right. People do use the fountain. The day care is using it now. Not to drink from, though. They're turning the fountain into a sprinkler. A very orderly group. They take turns spraying each other. I wonder if their thumbs are cleaner than the dog's tongue.

"Disgusting!" says the old man again, standing up slowly and shuffling away. When he stands up, a piece of litter falls out of his pocket. Crumpled paper. It skitters towards me in the wind.

I hate litter. "Hey!" I say. I grab the piece of paper and run after the old man. "Excuse me," I say, "but this is yours. Do you want it?"

Stooped as he is, he's about my height. He doesn't look at the piece of paper. He looks straight at me. His mouth turns down naturally. "You keep it," he says, "if you care so much about it." He turns around and shuffles off.

I go back to Sally and Frieda.

"Where'd you get that?" Frieda asks.

"The old guy dropped it. He said I could keep it. What a grouch."

"What's grouchy about giving away money?" asks Frieda.

I examine the litter for the first time. It's a five-dollar bill. I'm not used to American money. It isn't very colorful. I'd recognize a blue Canadian five-dollar bill right away. I look up for the old man, but he's vanished into the crowd.

"What'll we do with the money?" I ask.

"He told you to keep it, didn't he?" says Frieda. "So let's keep it. With five dollars we can take a cab to my place."

6

The Best Ice Cream in the World

Lots of cabs pass by the park gates, but none of them wants to stop for us. I'm waving my arms. Frieda and Sally wait nearby. Sally has her head in Frieda's lap. Frieda's stroking the dog's head, pulling her ears, crooning to her. The dog turns her head on one side, and licks Frieda's hand, then sneezes gently.

"The thing is," Frieda says quietly, "that I won't be allowed to keep you. No way Mom is going to be happy with a dog in the house."

– *You don't know that,* says Norbert.

Frieda sighs, and strokes. Her designer outfit is a lot dirtier than it was a half hour ago.

"I know," she says. "Trust me, I know."

– No, you trust me. After all, on Jupiter tomorrow is Trustday.

"Trustday?" I say.

A motorized wheelchair pulls up near us. A bulky man inside, with huge arms and no legs. Friendly guy, with a big smile for Frieda and a smaller one for me.

"Should be along any minute now," he says.

"What should?" I ask.

"Why, the bus of course," he says. "Takes you right up Central Park West."

We're waiting by a bus stop. I hadn't noticed. "Oh," I say.

Sally is sniffing around a lamppost.

"That your dog?" the man asks. "Should be on a leash, you know. Most dogs'll dash out into traffic and get themselves run over. Big city's no place for a dog unless it's awfully smart."

"Sally's pretty smart," says Frieda.

– That's what you think, says Norbert. *Get back from that, Sally, it's disgusting!*

The man frowns at Frieda, then at Sally. A bus pulls up and stops. Regular-looking bus, except that it has extra-wide middle doors. The driver stops so that these doors are near us. Then the strangest thing happens. With a sigh of escaping air, the bus – all ten tons of it – sinks down until the doors are level with the sidewalk. There's something old-fashioned about the gesture, like an elephant going down on its wrinkly knees before a rajah. The wide middle doors open, and the bulky man wheels himself onto the bus. The driver is there to help. He beckons.

And, in a kind of dream sequence, we get on the bus too.

"Cash or card!" the driver shouts. We're almost the only ones on the bus. The bulky man takes out a plastic card. "Three dollars!" the driver shouts at us. He's got the name TED stitched on his shirt pocket. "Three dollars for the two of you. Not my fault – I don't set the rates."

The bulky guy wedges himself near the middle doors and hangs on to a handrail. I hold out our money. "No change!" shouts the driver. "Not my fault – they won't let me carry any."

"I've got change," says the bulky guy. He pulls some bills from a wallet in his shirt pocket. "Let me see that Lincoln there."

I don't know what he's talking about. "Lincoln?" I say.

Frieda sighs. "The five-dollar bill," she explains. "It's got a picture of Abraham Lincoln on it."

No kidding. I take a quick peek as I hand it over. Hairy guy with a beard. I get five one-dollar bills. Another hairy guy on them, only this guy has no beard. Ted the bus driver takes three of the bills and jogs up to the front of the bus. "Next stop, 62nd Street!" he shouts over his shoulder. I sit down near Frieda.

The bus starts forward with a jerk. Frieda rolls into the bulky guy, who grabs her chair with his free arm. Sally lets out a startled yip, and slides backwards along the floor. Behind us, other drivers jam on their brakes and hit their horns. Ted waves out his open window. "Stupid transmission. Not my fault!"

The sun peeps from behind a cloud, as if unsure if it's safe to come out yet. We crawl uptown, horns honking around us. Time passes. People get on and off the bus. Some of them stare at us. Some don't. I begin, slowly, to relax. We're on our way now. Soon we'll be at Frieda's place. I'll find out what happened to Dad this morning. I hope he'll be proud of me. I hope he'll be ashamed of himself.

The bulky guy reaches down to stroke Sally behind the ears.

"I have a dog, at home," he says. "A Jack Russell terrier. I'm teaching him tricks. Does your dog do tricks?"

"Not really," says Frieda.

"My little pooch will roll over when I tell him, and fetch a ball. I'm working on getting him to bark on command. Maybe your dog isn't as smart as mine."

Frieda doesn't say anything.

"Speak!" says the man, snapping his fingers in front of Sally's nose.

Ted shouts, "78th Street," and swings the bus towards the curb. I haven't been paying attention for a while. Last intersection I remember was 72nd. Anyone who can count can get around in New York. There are buildings on both sides of the street now, smaller and somehow friendlier buildings than they were a few blocks ago.

"Speak!" says the man again.

Sally puts her head on one side. Norbert sighs.

– Yes, what is it? Normally I don't like to be interrupted in my studio. Piero della Francesca felt the same way.

The bulky guy grips the arm of his chair. Hard.

– *Though, now that I think of it, maybe you can help me. What color hair does the sky have today?*

"What on earth . . ." the man begins. Norbert goes on.

– *That's just the point. On Earth. Now, on Jupiter, where I come from, the sky is usually a blonde or brunette, depending on the weather. Today, for instance, would be dark brunette weather, with a chance of ringlets.*

The man stares at Sally in horror.

– *The instructions on my paints say the product is suitable for summer treated color – but summer color could be anything from beach bangles to a tornado bouffant. Just last year I saw a redhead before Labor Day. Would you believe it? You never used to see redheads until Thanksgiving. Probably something to do with cosmetology or global warming.*

"What's he talking about?" Frieda asks me in a low voice.

"I have no idea."

The bulky guy takes out a magazine from a pouch at the side of his chair. He holds it up in front of his face. The pages tremble.

The bus comes to a sudden stop. Traffic looks like a plate of gloppy spaghetti. "Hey!" says Ted, leaning out the window and honking on his horn. "Let's get a move on here!" Nothing happens, except the driver beside Ted calls him a bad name.

"Oh, look!" Frieda points behind us, on the far side of the road. A corner restaurant with a patio. "I know that place," she says. "They make the best ice cream there. It is *so* not bad. But . . . it's not on Central Park West." She slides up her sunglasses to see better. "*We're* not on Central Park West," she says.

Ted hears her, and turns round in his chair. "This is Amsterdam," he says. "Didn't I call it out? There's construction at the top end of the park. They're routing everyone over this way. That's why the traffic is so bad."

And that's why there are buildings on both sides of the street.

"Do you want to get off?" he asks.

"Let's," says Frieda. "Come on, Alan."

The bus kneels again. Sally jumps out on her own. I help Frieda. Traffic isn't moving at all. Ted shakes his head at it before closing the middle doors. "What a mess!" he says.

– *Don't worry,* says Norbert. *It's not your fault.*

Frieda is right. It is the best ice cream in the world.

We're sitting at an outdoor table, under the sign that says DAIRY DREAM. Frieda is sitting in a plastic chair, her wheelchair pushed over against a railing. I'm in a plastic chair too. Sally is resting underneath the table, gnawing tiredly on the end of a sugar biscuit. The sun is out, for now. Still lots of clouds in the sky.

My two dollars, plus the money in Frieda's purse, was just enough to buy us each a scoop of cinnamon ice cream. Cinnamon is her favorite. The ice cream came in a silver bowl, with a big sugar biscuit. I didn't want to give my biscuit to Sally, but Frieda insisted.

The waitress sees what we are doing, and comes back outside with a plateful of sugar biscuits in her wrinkled hand. "For the doggie," she says.

I'm feeling almost happy – a combination of the sun, and the ice cream, and the fact that Frieda's place is only a few blocks away. We can walk it easily.

"Won't they be surprised to see me with you!" I say.

She's twiddling one of her earrings. She doesn't answer.

"You sure you don't want to phone?" I ask. "There's a phone here."

She shakes her head. "I phoned from the airport, on my cell," she says. "But I couldn't get through. It's Monday – my mom's Tutankhamen Society day. The phone never stops ringing on Mondays." She grimaces.

"Tutankhamen – I remember him," I say. "He was a pharaoh, right? Egyptian, I mean. Like your earrings."

"Yeah." She doesn't sound that excited.

Parked on the side street next to us is a truck. I guess it was white when the paint was fresh. Now it's dust colored. A small truck with two back doors, both swung wide open, and a long narrow ramp down to the street.

– *I remember Tutankhamen too,* says Norbert. *Uncle Nathan told me about him. A nasty little boy.*

"Tutankhamen!" Frieda's face hardens. She swings her feet under the table. She has to concentrate to make them work. Sally whimpers.

– *Hey, watch it!*

"Oh, sorry!" Frieda bends down. "Did I kick you? I didn't mean to."

– *Yes, you did.*

"Well, I meant to kick something, but not you." Frieda strokes the dog's head. The dog licks her hand.

"Oh, I wish I could keep you," she says. "I wish I wish I wish."

Her sunglasses prevent me from seeing her eyes, but she sounds like she's about to cry.

– *Maybe you can,* says Norbert.

"I can't. I know I can't. Mother hates dogs."

– *This is Wishday,* says Norbert.

"Monday," Frieda says.

– *On Jupiter, Monday is Wishday. You never know what can happen on Wishday.*

"You mean Washday," I say. "Isn't that how the rhyme goes?"

– *Wishday. Make a wish on Monday. Trust it on Tuesday. Nerissa and I met on a Wishday,* he says, with a sigh.

"You never told me this stuff before," I say. "What other days of the week do you have?"

– *Let's see. Wishday, Trustday, and Restday are early in the week. Standday, Greenday, and Happyday are later. Fearday is an unlucky one; no one likes it. No one gets married on Fearday. You'd call it Fearday the thirteenth.*

"You could phone again," I say to Frieda. "You might get through this time."

It's rude to arrive unannounced. My mom told me that. She hates it when I bring a friend home and don't warn her.

"Call again," I say. "Please? Or you could leave a message. Does your place have an answering machine?"

She stares at me like I've asked if they have a toilet. "The memory holds only twenty messages. After twenty, you get a voice telling you to hang up and try your call again."

"Oh." I can't imagine anyone having twenty messages at once, before they can call back.

She snorts. "You are such a yokel, you know that, Alan?"

"I . . ." I stop. "Yokel?"

"You know." She rolls her eyes. "Bumpkin, rube, hayseed."

"These are insults, right?" I just want to be sure.

– *Nonsense. They're vegetables.* Norbert sounds nostalgic. *Ahh, the vegetables of Jupiter. I remember eating pickled rubes and buttered hayseeds when I was a little snifter.*

Sally has finished the biscuits. She yawns, showing some pretty nice-looking teeth.

Frieda sputters.

– *Mmm good. And then for dessert, my favorite: bumpkin pie. My mom makes a great bumpkin pie.* Norbert sniffs. Sally sneezes. Frieda laughs and laughs.

The waitress comes up to our table. "So nice to see young people laughing together," she says. "How was your ice cream?"

"Wonderful!" I say.

"I've seen you here before," the waitress says to Frieda. "You usually come with an older lady. But, you know, I think this is the first time I've seen you laugh."

Frieda looks embarrassed.

The waitress smiles. She's an older lady herself. Wrinkles all over her face, from the double chin all the way up to the hairnet. Her legs are bowed. She's wearing a stained apron. For a moment I think she's going to pinch my cheeks. Instead, she nudges my arm with her elbow. "She is laughing because she is with a young man like you. Heh-heh. Today she leaves her mother at home, and you make her laugh!"

My turn to be embarrassed.

Frieda isn't laughing now. "I don't come here with my mother," she says.

The waitress picks up our silver bowls and shuffles away.

A couple of kids go skateboarding by. One of them runs right up the ramp and into the parked truck. The ramp is metal, and makes a clatter. The kid skates back down. The other kid laughs.

They're both wearing baggy jeans and floppy hats and sunglasses. Their shirts ride high. The logo of a famous running shoe company proclaims itself from the waistband of their underpants. The kids skate down the street, heels high as they kick off.

I shrink inside my own clothes.

"I want to do that," says Frieda suddenly. She gets up from the table, swings herself into her chair, and rolls off the patio and down the sidewalk.

"What? Where are you going?"

Frieda finds the ramp at the street corner, and rolls herself along the side street towards the parked truck. She stops at the foot of the ramp, takes a deep breath, and begins to push herself up. She gets only a few feet up when one of her hands slips, and the chair slides down to the foot of the ramp. She shakes her head, and tries again. She gets halfway up the ramp, this time, working harder and harder. She slows. Slows some more. Stops.

"Let me help." I run over and stand beside the ramp, ready to grab hold of the chair.

"No," she says, breathing hard. "Get away!"

I take a step back. She lifts her hands and the wheelchair slides smoothly down the ramp and onto the street again. She rolls backwards a few seconds, then brakes. Her mouth is tight.

"Come on, Frieda," I say. "Let's get going. We can be at your place in a few minutes."

"First this," she says. She spits on her hands, takes a few deep breaths. Olympic weight lifters don't wear sunglasses during competition, but she has the same look on her face. Concentration. Going for the record.

The sun disappears behind a cloud.

A car drives past us, honking. Something about it looks familiar. Frieda ignores the car, rolls herself forward bending at the waist, her arms flashing back and forth as she takes short sharp pulls. She gains speed quickly.

The car reverses into a parking spot across the road.

Frieda is almost all the way up the ramp now. Her mouth is open. She's panting. Her arm muscles writhe like snakes. Can she do it?

I'm afraid she'll lose control at the top of the ramp. I remember riding my bike up a steep hill in Port Hope – that's next door to Cobourg, where I live; there are no hills in Cobourg – getting tireder and tireder as I got closer to the top, my pedals moving more and more slowly, until finally they stopped altogether. And I didn't have enough strength to get off the bike. I just fell over sideways, like a monkey falling out of a tree. Nearly got run over. I don't want that to happen to Frieda, so I run up the ramp myself just as she makes it to the top.

"Yes! Yes!" she cries, pumping her fist in the air.

I don't move as smoothly as Frieda or the skateboarders. My running jars the ramp loose, and it falls to the ground with a huge clatter just as I reach the top. I jump into the back of the truck.

"Yes, yes, yes!" She's still pumping her fist. Her face shines with joy and sweat. She's not paying attention to where she's going. Her chair rolls backwards. The road isn't too far to jump, but Frieda's not a jumper. I grab the back of her chair, and hang on like a bad cold. I don't want her rolling over the edge.

The truck engine starts, whirs a couple of times, and stops.

Someone's in the truck cab. I didn't hear anyone get in. The engine whirs and stops again.

Two men are crossing the road towards us. Did they come from the blue car? One of the men is slouchy; the other, skinny. I smell cologne.

Oh, no. No no no.

"I don't believe it," says Slouchy. He grabs one of the rear doors and swings it shut. There's a bolt at the bottom.

He locks the door tight. "After all the trouble we've had finding you. At the airport. Trying to follow your cab."

"Taking that old lady home," Skinny reminds him.

"Oh, yeah. What a lousy tipper she was! And now, just driving around your neighborhood, we find you waiting for us. I don't believe it."

Skinny holds the other door ready to slam. "Do you see how dirty this truck is?" he says. "Whoever owns it must not care what it looks like at all."

"I guess he won't mind us borrowing it, then," says Slouchy. He bangs on the side of the truck. "Hurry up, Ron, I thought you knew how to hot-wire these things."

Skinny slams the other rear door, leaving us in darkness.

The engine finally catches. The truck takes off. I fall over. Frieda's chair falls over.

What a mess.

7 What Would Norbert Do?

No windows in the back of the truck, but the darkness is not quite total. Chinks of light show through the door fittings. Frieda is sitting up on the floor, rubbing her hand. Her chair is nearby, on its side. "Are you all right?" I ask.

Brakes squeal. The truck turns sharply, throwing me against Frieda. Her chair slides past us. The top wheel is spinning.

Somewhere outside a dog is barking.

We realize what this means at the same time. "Where's Sally?" she asks.

"Where's Norbert?" I say.

We turn towards each other in the dimness. I don't know about Frieda, but I feel awfully alone. In a weird way Norbert is a link to reality for me. He's part of my past, part of the world of Mom and school, of my friends Victor and Miranda. I haven't thought about Miranda in a while. She's not a girlfriend, exactly, but she is a friend, and a girl.

Here I am in the dark with a different girl. Maybe that's why I'm thinking about Miranda now.

"Poor Sally!"

Is Frieda crying? The truck takes another turn, and she falls against me. Lots of dumb things come into your mind when you're in trouble. Frieda's hair smells nice. Sort of spicy. "What are we going to do?" she asks.

"I don't know."

The truck stops. I can hear the radio in the front playing loudly. I can hear traffic noises: horns blaring, brakes shrieking, motors burbling and growling. I scramble over to the door and try to open it from the inside. I find a handle and pull. Nothing happens. I push. Nothing happens.

The truck starts up again. I sit beside Frieda. We bump up and down for a bit.

"Are you really rich?" I say. "Is that why they're after you?"

"You're here too," she reminds me.

"Yes, but it's you they want," I say. I'm trying to convince myself that I'm okay, even though I know I'm not. I'm a witness. I've seen enough movies to know what happens to witnesses. Gulp.

"I think we're pretty rich," she says. "We have a cottage on the ocean, and a boat. I love the boat. Dad promised to take me sailing when I got back. I hope he's not too busy."

"My friend Victor has a sailboat," I say. "He and his dad go in races, every Wednesday night. They took me once." I fell overboard, and Victor kidded me about it for weeks. "It was pretty crowded, with the three of us," I say.

"A dinghy," she says, in a tone of voice that says dinghies are no good – only yokels have dinghies. "Our boat is a cutter. Forty-four feet long, with a crew of four."

The truck speeds up. Traffic noises are quieter.

My stomach rolls. I look at my watch. It's got a button at the side that turns on a light, so you can see the time even in the dark. 12:15. I think back to the ice cream. I wish I'd eaten the sugar cookie. I think back to breakfast, early this morning.

I have a sudden mental picture. I can see our kitchen counter, with the butter dish and toast crumbs. I see the jam spreading smoothly under my knife, savor the good feeling after I wipe the knife on the edge of the jar and it comes away clean.

"I'm hungry," I say. My stomach rolls again.

"You're scared."

I think about it. The truck makes a long turn. The wheelchair slides. We slide after it. "I'm hungry *and* scared," I say.

She doesn't seem scared. Not the way I'm scared. She's upset about Sally, and worried about something else – something other than Slouchy and Skinny. And Ron, whoever he is.

"Did you see the driver of the truck?" I ask. "The guy they called Ron?"

"No."

"Do you think they'll ask for a lot of ransom money?"

"Shut up."

"A million dollars?"

"Shut up, will you!"

I think about my mom, trying to find a million dollars. Dad would help too, but I don't think they'd be able to do it. Then they'd blame each other.

Frieda has her head down. Her shoulders are shaking. "Hey," I say. "Don't cry." Really good thing to say. She cries harder. The truck slows, and she falls over.

"Don't worry," I say. "I'm sure they'll find the money – your dad being an important politician, and the big boat and all. Oh, yeah. They'll find the money, no matter how much it is."

I'm doing really badly here. Frieda is crying harder than ever, crying so hard I'm kind of worried that she'll hurt herself. In the movies they slap people who cry like this, but I don't want to slap Frieda in case she slaps me back. I lift her up, so that we're sitting side by side, and I put my arm around her shoulder. She has big shoulders, like a couple of railroad ties.

Her crying calms down a bit. She yawns. "Suppose they . . . don't *want* to pay," she says.

Ooh.

"Sure, they have the money, but what if they don't want to spend it on *me?*"

Ooh. That's what she's worried about all along.

"I heard my mom talking on the phone about how expensive my operations were, how they weren't really worth it because I was still . . . *broken.*" Frieda pushes away from me, and makes her voice sound all bubbly. " 'Honestly, darling, all that money, all those operations to fix her, and the child is still broken. Who's ever going to care about her?' That's what Mom said."

"Yuck."

"Not unyuck," she agrees.

The truck stops suddenly. We both fall forward. The engine shuts off. I can't hear any traffic. The light is dimmer than it was; dimmer than it should be at – I check my watch – 12:50. I wonder where we are.

"Hello?" I knock on the side of the van. "Hello?"

"Quiet in there!" The voice is pitched high, and right next to the back door. I jump.

Is it Ron's voice? There's something familiar about it. I sit still for a moment. Nothing happens. Then a strange thought wanders into my head, a thought from another time, another place. A thought from another mind. *What would Norbert do?*

There were horrible bullies at my school last year. I was afraid of them. But Norbert wasn't. And when he laughed at the bullies, and called them names, I was scared, but I knew it was the right thing to do. "Help!" I shout. "Help help help!"

"Be quiet. Or else!" Ron – if it is Ron – sounds upset.

"Or else what? You going to take us for a ride?" I bang on the side of the truck. "Come on, Frieda! Make some noise! Help! Help! Help!"

Frieda shrieks – a pretty good one – it echoes around the inside of the truck. She's holding my hand. I don't mind. Two kids in the dark, screaming at the top of their lungs.

Ron tells us to be quiet again, but he sounds like he knows he can't make it stick. He sounds like a French teacher telling you to be quiet, or an out-of-town relative at a family picnic. The sort of guy you can ignore. And he's alone.

And then he isn't.

"What's going on?" asks Slouchy. I'd recognize his voice anywhere. "Any trouble?"

"No," says Ron.

"Good," says Slouchy.

Frieda gasps. I shut up. I can't help it, I'm scared.

Then I hear a rolling sound, like a skateboard, and another voice saying, "Thought I heard something." Not a kid's voice, but not grown-up. And what an accent. *Thwahwt I huwd somepm.*

"No," says Ron. "Just us talking."

"Sounded like someone calling for help," says the not-quite-grown-up voice. *Cwollin fuh heaylp.* It takes me a second to figure out what he's saying.

"Beat it, junior," says Slouchy. "And take your wagon with you."

Not a skateboard. Junior sounds too old to be playing with a wagon. "You sure there's no one calling for help?" he says.

"I didn't hear anything," says Slouchy. "You hear anything, Ron?"

"No," says Ron.

"You sure?" *Shew-ah,* it sounds like.

Silence. I should make a noise. I should say something.

That's what Norbert would do. I open my mouth, but nothing comes out except air.

"I told you to beat it," says Slouchy.

"Shew-ah." He doesn't seem too worried. The sound of his wagon fades in the distance. One of its wheels squeaks.

The doors of the truck open. There's Slouchy, with his red hair and cologne.

"Get out!" he says. "Jones, Ronnie, get them out!" Jones must be the real name of the skinny government guy. He might have superpowers at the airport; here he follows Slouchy's orders.

Hands reach towards us in the darkness. Ronnie's are small, delicate, with tinted nails. Ronnie is a woman. I'm so surprised, I forget my fear.

Frieda is nodding to herself. "I wondered, back at the airport," she says.

"Ron?" I say. "Ronnie? Veronica?"

The flight attendant. So interested in taking care of us, I remember. Wonder if she takes care of all her passengers this way, or if we're getting special treatment.

They hustle me out of the truck first. Then they lift Frieda down – not very carefully. I grab her before she falls over. Her designer suit is covered in grease and dirt. Her sunglasses are gone. Without them, she looks younger.

I help her to the ground. She sits with her back against a broken fence. She looks like a doll. Her head is on one side. Her eyes are wide open – startling blue eyes. I've never noticed them before. The same color as her earrings.

Her muscular arms dangle. You almost expect her to say, "Mama," or "I made wee-wee," or "Math is hard!"

"So we finally got you out of your chair, hey!" says Slouchy. "Couldn't do it in the airport. You were too clever, hey? Well, who's laughing now?" He is, that's who. I catch a faint glint of his silver tooth.

We're in an alley. Trash all over. Tall brick buildings blocking out the sky. Traffic noise very faint in the distance. Skinny stands next to me.

"Well, Ronnie?" Slouchy asks over his shoulder. Veronica is in the back of the truck. "Did you get them?"

I can't see what she's doing, but I hear a metallic clunking sound. Frieda's chair sliding along the floor.

"Have you heard from my parents?" Frieda asks. "What do they say?"

Veronica gets down from the truck, brandishing something wrapped in brown paper. There's a smell that takes me back to a summer's day long ago, when I was very small and my dad was treating the back fence. Creosote. It's also the smell of railroad ties – I wonder if I smelled it earlier. The package has been thoroughly waterproofed.

"What do my parents say?" Frieda asks. A brave girl. She's afraid of the answer, but she wants to know.

Slouchy's eyes are on the wrapped package. "I've never talked to your parents," he says.

"Then why," she gasps, "did you kidnap me?"

"Kidnap?" says Skinny. "Who said anything about kidnap?"

"It's not kidnapping to borrow a truck with two kids hiding in the back," says Slouchy. "And, anyway, we don't care about you. We wanted the wheelchair."

For a moment I think Frieda is going to cry.

Veronica unwraps the bundle carefully, and peers inside. "Old Hawkface is here," she says. "And in one piece. Earless will be happy to see him."

"He's waiting in the gallery. You take it to him, Jones. He'll want to clean it before showing it off." Slouchy stares at us, even though he's talking to Skinny. "Leave the truck someplace when you're done. Ronnie, you wait in the car. I won't be long." Parked at the end of the alley is the blue car with the pink tassel on the aerial.

"I'll take it to Earless," says Veronica, casually.

"Better let Jones do it. It's his gallery, after all."

I wonder who Hawkface is. And Earless. They sound like bad guys from a comic book.

Slouchy pushes me towards Frieda's fence. I sit down beside her. He slams the back doors of the truck. He doesn't bother with the bolt lock this time.

"What about Frieda's chair?" I ask. "She can't get around without it."

"She shouldn't have slapped me," he says, with a bully's sneer.

The car drives away. I notice an empty cigarette pack nearby. LUCKY, it says on the side. I don't feel lucky.

Slouchy comes over, and squats down beside us. A big strong mean man, with a cologne to match. "I'm going now," he says. "But I want you two kids to listen very carefully to what I have to say." His quiet conversational tone is scarier than yelling would be. "I want what happened here to be our little secret. Okay? If either of you ever – *ever* – tells anyone, I'm going to come and get you," he says. "I will find you. I will hurt you. I will hurt your family. I will hurt your dog."

"The dog isn't mine," I say. The words pop out before I can stop them. I'm so relieved to hear he's going that I can't help myself. "I don't have any pets. I used to have a turtle named Mr. Whiskers, but he crawled into the heating duct."

Slouchy doesn't say anything. He stares at me. I shut up.

"You never saw me," he begins again. "You don't know what I look like. You don't know what happened to the wheelchair. Is that a deal?"

"Sure," I say. Frieda nods.

"Are you going to talk to the police?"

"No," I whisper. Frieda shakes her head.

"Promise?"

"Promise."

"Good. I want you two to close your eyes now, and count to a thousand. Don't open your eyes until you reach a thousand. I'll be listening for you. Do you understand?"

I nod. My eyes are closed. "One, two three four," I say.

"Don't start yet," he says.

"Sorry," I say.

I hear him move away. "Start . . . now," he says.

"One, two, three, four," I say. Frieda is shivering against me. If she's counting, she's doing it awfully quietly.

"Louder!" he calls, from farther away.

"Five six seven eight," I say. "Nine ten eleven twelve."

I'm on seven hundred and thirty-eight when I hear panting next to my ear.

– *Ready or not, here I come!* says Norbert.

8

Bird

I open my eyes slowly, one at a time. The car with the pink tassel on the aerial is gone. Apart from trash, and us, the alley is empty.

Sally is licking Frieda's face. Frieda has her arms around the dog's neck.

"You found us!" I say. "Hey, great!" I pat the dog on the back. "Way to go, Sally!" I say. "Good tracking."

– *I helped.* Norbert sounds petulant.

"Good for you too," I tell him. "Did you guys have a tough time finding us?"

– *Yes.* Norbert doesn't elaborate. *Say, Frieda, where's your chair?*

"We can't go yet. We're supposed to count to a thousand," I say.

– *That's some serious game of hide-and-seek,* says Norbert.

Is it safe? Are they gone? I stand up, cramped from all my time on the ground. Away down at the end of the alley, traffic is passing. A car backfiring sounds like a gunshot. Frieda screams. I drop to the ground and close my eyes.

"Seven hundred and thirty-nine," I say in a loud voice. "Seven hundred and forty. Seven hundred and forty-one."

– *Enough with the counting! Anyone would think this was math class.*

I stay down. Nothing happens for a couple of minutes. It seems silly to keep my eyes closed. I open them in time to see a dog trot around the corner, stop, and then come towards us, growling softly. A really big dog, brown and black, with proud shoulders and a heavy head. A boss dog. An emperor among dogs.

Sally jumps away from Frieda and stands as tall as she can. Her tail, which has been moving back and forth like a fan, is still.

– *Oh, no,* says Norbert.

The boss dog trots forward. One of his ears is gone. His teeth are all there though. He shows them. Sally stands her ground, bristling and growling.

– *Come on, now, girl,* says Norbert. *We don't want another scene like the one with the poodle on the way here, do we?*

Sally growls. The boss dog growls. I don't think they're happy to see each other.

"Do you think that big ugly dog will hurt Sally?" Frieda asks.

"I don't know."

"Shouldn't we be doing something? Shouting? Getting between them?"

"I don't want to get between them," I say.

– *You know, anyone who invents a breath mint for dogs is going to make a ton of money,* Norbert comments. *Hey, there, big boy, how about backing out of range, if you get me. Ten feet or so would do the trick.*

The dog puts his head on one side. Not coyly. More like he's deciding when to jump.

– *Now then, I wonder what your name would be,* says Norbert. *Could it be – Cuddles? Bubbles? No, too friendly. How about Marjoribanks? Featherstonaugh? No, too hard to spell. Oh, dear, I'm afraid we're left with stereotypes. Rex? Not quite. Something a little more patrician. Maybe – no, wait, I've got it. Caesar. Down, Caesar!* says Norbert. The dog, who has been sniffing at Sally, takes a step back and sits down.

– *Good dog. I guess Caesar is your name. A dumb name it is, too,* says Norbert.

The dog growls.

– *Caesar! That's no name for a dog. It's a name for a salad.*

The dog barks.

– *Quiet, Caesar!* Norbert laughs. *Quiet, you little bowl of lettuce! Quiet, or I'll pour some more dressing on you. And while we're on the subject of personal appearance, has anyone ever spoken to you about drooling? It's not required behavior, you know. It's optional. You don't have to – hey!!*

He's interrupted in mid-insult. Caesar jumps right past Sally, and keeps moving. I turn and see something out of a nursery rhyme. There's a cat running down the alley away from us. And in the cat's mouth is a rat. I don't know if there's any cheese in the rat's mouth.

Caesar moves fast towards the cat, who notices him at the last moment, jumps for the fence and, in her panic, drops the rat, who sits there in the middle of the alley. The dog stops in front of the rat, then decides he'd rather get the cat, so he leaps for the fence. He misses the cat, then takes off after the rat, who is disappearing quickly down the alley. Everybody's safe.

"What happened with the poodle on the way here?" I ask.

– *You don't want to know,* says Norbert.

"If we're going to get to my place," says Frieda, "we'll have to get to the street."

I help her to her feet. She sways like a poplar in a high wind.

– *What happened to the wheelchair?*

"They took it," I say. "And left us."

– *Those meanies!* says Norbert. *Wait until you tell the police!*

I catch Frieda's eye. I know what she's thinking. I'm thinking the same thing. No police. We don't say anything about it. "Come on," I say. Frieda puts her arm around my shoulders, and we hobble forward.

It's slow going. Sally runs ahead, turns around, stops. We hobble some more.

– *Is this our best plan?* asks Norbert. *Because at this rate, by the time we get back to Frieda's place, she'll be old enough to vote.*

We hobble on. I trip Frieda, and catch her just in time. "Sorry," I say.

"Uh-huh," she says.

"Caught my foot in your cuff. I'm afraid your pantsuit is going to need to go to the cleaners."

"Uh-huh," she says.

Strangely enough, I think she looks better now. More real, somehow, in her wrecked pantsuit, without her sunglasses and cell phone and with her hair all messed.

"Imagine Veronica working with Slouchy," I say.

"I know. She was so helpful before the flight, with the chair and all. It makes me mad."

– *Aren't you done playing with that, yet?* says Norbert. *Put it down, Sally. It stinks.*

I look over. Sally is carrying the piece of brown wrapping paper in her mouth. I reach down, awkwardly, take the paper away from the dog, and stick it in my pocket. An automatic gesture.

We keep walking. I never realized laneways were so long. I can see the street up ahead, but it's not moving closer.

We're approaching an intersection – another laneway cuts across ours. Frieda tightens her grip on my shoulder. "How're you doing?" I ask her. Norbert answers.

– *Fine, thanks. I'm having a little trouble keeping up to you guys. I think I'll put in a phone call to the Olympic committee. See if there's an opening for the fifty-foot hobble.*

"How about you?" I ask Frieda.

"Fine," she says in a little voice. "Thirsty, maybe."

"Boy, do I wish you hadn't said that," I say.

"You too, huh?"

"Well," I say, "I'm not unthirsty."

"You're getting the hang of this," she says. "Not bad for you."

Sally stops dead. Her big bat ears are perked forward.

"What's that noise?" asks Frieda. Wheels rolling unevenly towards us, with a squeak every second or two. One of the axles needs some oil. Sally dashes ahead to the intersection, then comes trotting back to report.

– *A wagon full of junk,* says Norbert.

The sound of the wheels gets louder. We wait. Around the corner of the laneway comes a teenager, pulling a wagon. He's a bit bigger and older than I am. He has baggy pants like the kids uptown, but his pants are ripped and there's no sportswear logo anywhere. His sunglasses wrap around his head. His cap is flat and square with no brim, like an upside-down sandwich container, only it's not made of plastic. His T-shirt has lightning bolts on it. He's smiling.

"How you doing?" he says.

"Fine," I say. I recognize the voice. "You were here a while ago. We were in the truck."

"Shew-ah," he says. He doesn't mention Slouchy warning him off.

I introduce us. "And Sally," I say, pointing at the dog.

He tells us his name: Boyd. He doesn't say if it is his first name or last name. He nods to each of us, including Sally. Acts completely unsurprised to see us.

"Hi, Boyd," I say.

"Hi, Bird," says Frieda.

Bird, not Boyd. He just pronounces it *Boyd.* I blush.

– *Hi,* says Norbert.

Bird doesn't blink. He nods. "Talkin' dog," he says.

"Nice wagon," I say.

"Shew-ah," he says. "Found it round a corner from here. Like I found my shoes." He's wearing a pair of nearly new trainers. He gazes off into the distance as he talks, like he sees things that aren't there.

"Um, Bird," I say. "We need your help. Frieda can't walk. She used to have a wheelchair, but she lost it."

He looks at her. "Red-haired guy with the truck?" he asks. She nods.

– *And the cologne,* says Norbert. *Don't forget the cologne.*

Bird smiles. "Funny talkin' dog," he says.

"Could Frieda ride in your wagon?" I say. "Not for very long. Just until . . ." and then I stop. I was going to say, "Until we get a cab." But I realize we don't have enough money for a cab. We don't have enough money for a phone call. We have just about enough for a drink of water at a fountain. Of course, there's no fountain around here. I swallow. "Not for long," I say.

Bird shoves some small metal pieces – of what: engine? radio? skateboard? – out of the way, to make room for

Frieda. She sits uncomfortably, with her legs splayed out. She hangs on tight to the sides of the wagon.

Bird is frowning. "You'll be wantin' a lift uptown," he says. "A cab, maybe."

"Maybe," I say.

"Be expensive." Frieda coughs, and opens her mouth, but before she can say anything, Bird continues. "I don't got much money," he says. "What I got is *things*. Cabs don't take things. They want money. I can't give you much."

Frieda shuts her mouth tight.

"You know, I never been uptown," says Bird. His eyes are faraway again.

– *Today is Wishday. Come with us,* says Norbert.

Around the corner of the alley, we find a big bottle of water. The seal is unbroken. Drops of condensation bead on the clear plastic sides of the bottle. Bottled water, resting there, waiting for us. Just like Bird's wagon.

Everyone takes a drink. I pour some water into a metal dish from the wagon. The dish smells of oil, but Sally laps thirstily. Now I can't believe how hungry I am. I must have been hungry all along, but I didn't pay any attention to it. If your hair is on fire, you don't care that you're running down Main Street in your underwear. Once the fire is out, you feel embarrassed.

I'm walking beside the wagon, helping Frieda to stay in. I offered to pull, but Bird wouldn't let me. "My wagon," he said.

We come around the next corner and onto the street. Is there a picnic waiting there, just for us? There is not. What there is is a minivan, with New Jersey licence plates and a flat front tire. Inside the van is a woman with her head in her hands. We crowd around her window. Sally jumps up and down. "Can we help?" I ask.

The lady is wearing a kerchief and sunglasses. She takes one look at us and screams.

9

Never Been Anywhere Else

With a jack that he finds in his wagon-load of scrap metal, Bird has the tire off the van in no time flat – ha-ha – and the spare – the little one, like a baby tire – out from under the back. Frieda hands him tools.

The street we're on has potholes and manholes and hoardings. Also stores with roll-down shutters, people walking in a hurry, seagulls eating trash. Two bridges take up a lot of the sky. One of them floats in the air, looking like it's going to take off any minute. In the distance, more people, bigger buildings. It's a hard busy landscape, even with the floating bridge. Not a tree, not a shrub, not a blade of grass.

"Where are we?" I ask Bird.

"Home," he answers, tightening bolts.

"Do you know where we are, Norbert?"

– *This is still Earth, isn't it? The sign over there says* MARKET STREET.

"Really?" I was kind of hoping it would be another famous road, like Broadway or Fifth Avenue. There's a Market Street in Cobourg, right behind Victoria Hall. You can get pretty good sausage there on Saturday mornings, when the farmers sell from the backs of their pickup trucks. Good vegetables too, my mom says, but who cares about vegetables? The best brussels sprouts in the world are still pretty bad.

"Do you know Market Street?" I ask Frieda.

She shrugs. "Lower East Side, isn't it?" she says. "I've never been down here before."

Bird smiles. "I never been anywhere else."

The lady in the van is warming up to us. She waves at us from time to time. When the spare tire is on, and the bolts are tightened, she drives away, still waving. I'm obscurely disappointed. Frieda is cast down too. Bird seems philosophical, picking up the handle to the wagon, stepping forward.

Norbert is not philosophical.

– *That's the thanks we get?*

I can't resist. "We?" I say. "What did you do?"

– *I hope she runs over broken glass,* he says, as the van turns a corner. *Or giant spikes. I hope she runs over spikes and pops all her tires at once. I hope she gets a speeding ticket. I've never seen such narrow selfishness. She's from New*

Jersey, isn't she? Typical. I could tell the moment I saw her, those beady little New Jersey eyes. Everything from New Jersey is little. Little eyes, little ears, and teeny-weeny hearts.

He stops at the sound of a tentative honk. The van is back. It must have gone around the block, then returned to our side. The lady opens the sliding side door with a flick of a driver-side button. Her smile is small and apologetic, like a puppy that's made a mistake on the living-room carpet. She asks if we need a lift anywhere.

We all say thank you, one after the other, like a row of parrots. Even Norbert murmurs something. The lady thanks us for changing the tire, and apologizes for her bad manners. "I'm just so scared of driving in the city. I usually come here with my husband, but he's away on business; this is my first time by myself. I got lost coming off the Manhattan Bridge, and then I got the flat tire. After you fixed it, all I wanted to do was find the Holland Tunnel and get home. I drove away, but I was too ashamed to keep going."

– *Ah, New Jersey. The generosity state,* Norbert says.

She frowns at us, unable to figure out who is speaking.

"I think we call ourselves the Garden State," she says.

– *Generosity is a plant that should be in every garden,* says Norbert.

Bird and I lift Frieda into the middle seat.

"Oh, my dear, I didn't see you were hurt," says the lady.

"I'm not," says Frieda.

Bird's wagon fits into the well by the side door. He climbs into the front seat. The lady from New Jersey is nervous with him beside her, a teenager with ripped ragged clothes. I sit with Frieda. Sally is in the back.

Frieda gives her address on West 84th Street – our destination for the past four hours. The New Jersey lady asks how to get there. Frieda doesn't know.

"What?" I ask. "But it's where you live."

"I know it's off Central Park West. But I've never had to get there on my own from way down here. I get driven most places." She looks down at her legs.

"Sorry," I say.

"What about you?" the New Jersey lady asks me. "Do you know how to get there?"

"Sorry," I say again.

"Don't mind the apologies. He's from Canada," Frieda explains.

Bird, of course, is no good to us. He's never been out of the neighborhood. He knows that Central Park is somewhere up that way. He points vaguely ahead.

A van full of people, and none of us knows the way.

"I'm from Jersey," says the lady. "I wouldn't be here, except that my sister is finally getting a divorce from her no-good husband, and wanted a shoulder to cry on."

"Central Park is the biggest green space inside city limits anywhere in the world," says Frieda.

"Maybe we'll be able to find it then," says the lady, putting the van in gear. "If we go too far, we can take you home to Canada," she says to me. She has slick dark hair and bulging eyes. Her clothes are mostly green. She looks like a worried frog. "And, please," she adds, "children, keep your eyes open for gas stations. The spare tire is only a temporary replacement."

"So this is Park Avenue," I say, after we've been on it for a quarter of an hour or so. "When do we get to the park?"

"I don't know." The lady – whose name is Mrs. Amboy – drives slowly among the limousines and yellow cabs and buses, which seem to make up most of the traffic. We see a lot of different tail lights as they pass us, one set at a time.

I stare up ahead. Blocks and blocks of tall buildings, blotting out all of the sky except a narrow blue strip. Park Avenue seemed like the right street to turn onto. Back then the cross streets had numbers like 15 and 16. Now we're up to 65, and still no sign of a park. Mind you, we passed streets named Canal and Mulberry without seeing water or fruit.

"Turn left," says Frieda suddenly. "I've been here before."

A left-pointing arrow directs us right through the middle of Central Park. On the other side of the park is a street I recognize from Ted's bus ride. We must be nearly there.

"Keep going," says Frieda. "Then take the next right. There's construction on Central Park West."

"Oh, yeah," I say.

Ten minutes later we're in front of Frieda's house.

Actually, we're four doors down, in the only empty parking spot on the block. Mrs. Amboy turns around to stare at Frieda. "You live here?"

"Uh-huh."

"A real Manhattan brownstone," she says. "I must tell my husband."

"Uh-huh," says Frieda. She's not paying attention, I can tell. She frowns up at the house, and then back at Sally.

I don't understand why Mrs. Amboy is so excited about the houses. They're not brownstones – not now. They're sooty dirty graystones. And what's so impressive about them? Big old places with no front yards, on a noisy street. A kid in my class at school lives in a house like this – and we feel sorry for him. Frieda's is the one with the wooden ramp zigzagging up to the front door.

Sally is first out of the van. She disappears around the back of a car parked half on the sidewalk. We thank Mrs. Amboy again as we get out. She waves, closes the door with a click of her button, and drives off. The faster traffic parts and flows around her like a swiftly moving stream around a boulder.

I'm so relieved I could faint. We've made it. Made it.

Frieda's frowning. "Alan, we need to have a plan now."

"Why? We're home. You live here. I can call my dad. We're safe," I say. "Aren't we?"

"Safe? I suppose so. We have to make a plan about Sally. My mom will hit the roof if I bring a dog home. We've got to find a way to hide her."

"Ah."

"The first question is, do we tell Beatrice? That's my nanny."

I think a minute. "Was she supposed to meet you at the airport?"

"Uh-huh."

"And I guess she's the older lady who takes you for ice cream?"

Frieda nods.

"Then don't tell her," I say.

"Why not?"

"Because she doesn't make you laugh. A secret like this is something for people who make you laugh."

She raises her eyebrows. "That's pretty good," she says. "You're not always as stupid as you look, kid . . . I mean, Alan."

"Thanks. I think."

"But what am I going to do? I really . . . oh, I *really* want to keep her."

Sally slouches up to the wagon. Puts her head in Frieda's lap. Frieda puts her arms around the dog and squeezes hard.

"Where were you?" I ask. "What was so exciting behind the car there?"

– *Fire hydrant,* says Norbert curtly.

Bird stands in the middle of the sidewalk looking up and down and all around. The street is cleaner than the one he is used to; the buildings are better kept, the cars are nicer looking. The same steam pours out of the manholes.

Frieda looks up from the dog to stare at me. "What'll I do?" she asks, a girl with a dirty face and ripped clothes, sitting in a wagon heaped with junk.

I don't have a real answer. "Wait and see," I say.

"Do you think *you* could hide Sally in the house?" she asks me. "Hey! There's an idea! I'll distract Beatrice, and you find a place for the dog."

"Me?" I say.

"My mom's Tutankhamen Society will be meeting in the living room. Don't try there. Or the kitchen. Beatrice is usually there. Try my bedroom."

"You mean me?"

"Yes, my bedroom will be the best place. It's the third – no, the fourth – room on the left. Don't make any noise, though."

"You're still talking about *me*?"

She frowns. "And sometimes you are every bit as stupid as you look."

Bird pulls the wagon along the sidewalk, towards the ramp. "You okay?" he asks her.

"Fine," she says. Her mouth is closed in a thin line.

The lady who opens the front door is short, chubby, and tearfully happy. She wears an apron over plain dark clothes, and smells of furniture polish. All of which lead me to suspect that she is not Frieda's mom.

"Oh, *MadredeDio*," she says, or something like that, running the words into one and clasping her small red chapped hands together. "It is you, my little one." She runs forward, ignoring me and Bird and the dog and the dirty wagon, bending down to throw her arms around Frieda.

Even though I have a mission, hiding Sally, and even though I'm not the one being hugged, I find myself relaxing. The immediate threat is over.

– *Pssst, Dingwall. Let's go!* Norbert knows what I'm supposed to do.

Beatrice is still weeping into Frieda's shoulder. Frieda makes angry shooing gestures at me behind her nanny's back. Bird watches the whole thing with the biggest smile on his face. I grab the dog and walk into the house.

A large square hall with flowers and statues and wood paneling. A smell of sweet smoke coming from somewhere. Stairs off to the left. Voices off to the right. A high-ceilinged corridor ahead of me. I don't have much time. I run down the corridor counting doors, feeling like a burglar or a secret agent. The fourth room has two glass doors. A big room. I open the doors. Sally runs past me.

It can't be a bedroom – too many chairs and no bed. A lot of books on shelves running all the way along one wall. A marble table in the middle of the room, with chairs grouped around it and a huge stone planter in the center. A photograph of the Sphinx on the wall.

The smell is stronger. Sweet-smelling smoke spirals up from a brass doodad on the floor. The lights are low. The drapes are closed.

I look around for Sally, but she's gone. I go out in the hall. She's not there either.

"Sally!" I hiss. A good name for hissing. "Norbert! Where are you?"

No reply.

Well, I was told to hide the dog, and I've hidden the dog. I can hear voices from the front hall. Time to go.

Beatrice has her hands on her hips. She has big dark soft eyebrows, which arch downwards now. Her eyes are wet. Her lipstick is smeared. Frieda is rubbing some off her cheek.

"But how did you get here?" Beatrice is asking. "Your plane was early? You look untidy. And *where* . . ." she shakes her head in utter incomprehension ". . . *where* is your chair?"

"Early?" I say, joining the group. "What do you mean, the plane was early? It was right on time."

Beatrice stares at me without seeing me. Then she returns to Frieda. "You are all right? You are safe? Tell me you are safe." In Beatrice's black eyes, the tears look like treacle.

"I'm okay," Frieda tells her.

"Are you sure, little one?"

"Of course I'm sure. I'm home now, aren't I?"

10

Like Bruce Willis

Beatrice roots around inside a big hall closet – good place for hiding a dog, if I'd noticed it – and pulls out a wheelchair. It looks like the other one, only a bit smaller. Frieda takes a deep breath and swings her legs around to the side of the wagon. Beatrice settles her into the chair with the ease of much practice.

"Well, well, look who's home!"

And here she is. Frieda's mom is a striking woman, posed in the doorway, one hand on her hip and the other out beside her. Her head is pointing to one side, making her look two-dimensional – all on one plane. Taller than my dad, with a beehive hat making her look even taller, draped in a black something or other from neck to ankle, she looks a lot like Snow White's wicked stepmother. She brings the sweet smoky smell with her.

"Frieda, my dear." Her voice is deep for a woman, and husky. "We weren't expecting you so soon. I'm afraid you've picked an awkward time to arrive. The Tutankhamen Society is just about to start our meeting."

"Yeah," says Frieda. Her voice sounds pale and pinched. "Here I am, though."

Mrs. Miller moves her head very slowly, until it's in profile on the other side. "And what have you been playing at? You're quite dirty, my dear. You'll want to change right away, I should say. Are you two boys acquaintances of Frieda's?"

"Shew-ah," says Bird. He takes off his sunglasses, smiles up at her.

"Yes, ma'am," I say. "We met in the –"

But she cuts me off. "I really must be going," she says. "Professor Malchus will be addressing the society as soon as he finishes at the buffet. The poor man arrived late. He has an absolutely unique artifact to tell us about. Apparently, it supports a theory he . . . yes, dear?"

"Mother, we're hungry," Frieda says. "We haven't eaten lunch yet."

Mrs. Miller sighs theatrically, and raises her arm to her forehead. "Very well. Please arrange your refreshment as quietly as possible, and eat in the kitchen. Frieda, my dear, I'm *so* glad to see you."

She turns in the doorway, and stalks sideways down the hall and into the room with the other voices. Frieda opens her mouth to call after her, then closes it again. I can sympathize. My mom doesn't have a lot of time for me either.

"What did she mean, about not expecting you until later?" I whisper. Frieda shrugs.

"Come in," says Beatrice. "All of you. You must be starved! The kitchen is this way." She leads us down the corridor. Frieda wheels herself forward. "Where did you hide Sally?" she whispers.

I shrug my shoulders. "I don't know," I say.

There's a warning rumble from outside. Thunder.

I call my dad again, while Beatrice makes lunch.

"Marketing Department. Mr. Dingwall's office." A secretary's voice – calm, efficient, not very interested.

"Hi," I say. "My name is Alan Dingwall. I'm Mr. Dingwall's son."

"Well, hello, there. What can I do for you?"

"I was kind of hoping you could tell me where my dad is."

"Your dad's in a meeting right now, Alan. With some very important clients. He'll be sorry he missed your call. I know he's looking forward to seeing you later today."

"Later?"

"That's what he said. You are coming *today*, aren't you? Did he get the date wrong?"

"No, no. It's today. I mean, I'm here today."

"Good. I'll tell your dad you called, okay, Alan? And he'll see you later."

"Um," I say.

"Bye, then." She hangs up.

I hang up. I don't know what else to do.

I'm all on my own, and I don't like it. I'd like to like it. I should be having the time of my life. I should be enjoying myself more. I'm always telling my mom to let me do more on my own, and here I am, in the middle of a real adventure, and all I want is to go home.

Why can't I be more heroic? It looks easy in the movies.

The kitchen phone is in an alcove, with a mirror at eye level. I stare at myself. I try to cock one eyebrow, the way Bruce Willis does. Can't quite get it.

"Lunch is ready," calls Beatrice.

There's a place for me at the table: place mat, glass of milk, and a plate of sandwiches.

"Thanks very much," I say to Beatrice. She smiles.

I bite into my sandwich. Spiced meat and strong cheese on a crusty roll. It's really good.

Why can't I be more like Bruce Willis? My favorite part in his adventure movies is when the hero, having gone through flood, fire, and flying glass, finally dispatches all the villains, changes his shirt, and walks down the street to get a hug from his wife or girlfriend. And she asks how his day went, and he cocks one eyebrow and says something like "Routine," or "It wasn't boring." I love that. He doesn't want to make a big deal out of being a world saver. He is so Not Uncool. Even more not uncool than the kids on the skateboards.

I eat three sandwiches; also two glasses of milk, and a bunch of deep-fried pastry things that Beatrice calls *cannoli*. Bird eats well too.

Frieda is describing our morning's adventures to Beatrice, who is shaking her head and saying things in . . . I guess it's Italian. I don't know the language, but Beatrice is easy to follow. She's saying whatever the Italian is for *Holy Cow*, and *Isn't that awful*, and *Oh, you poor thing*.

Bird points at the last *cannoli*. "You want?" he asks.

I gesture for him to take it.

"You all right?" he asks me.

"Me? Oh, yeah," I say, as heartily as I can. "I'm just fine."

"You don't look fine," says Bird.

I sigh. I don't feel fine. Mom was right about Dad. Maybe she was right about me too. Maybe I'm not ready for too much independence.

Frieda goes off to change her clothes. Beatrice collects the dirty dishes and puts them in the dishwasher. Bird and I wander over to the big kitchen window and stare up. The sky is filling up with clouds. A big gray one drifts by. Looks like an airplane coming in to land. The thought gives me goose bumps. This seems like a good opportunity to do something I've been meaning to do for a while. "By the way, uh, Bird," I say. "I want to thank you for helping us."

He keeps looking out the window. "It was nice of you to let Frieda use your wagon," I say. "And to fix the lady's van. We'd never have made it here without you."

"Shew-ah," he says, the way he usually says it. Sure. Routine. I stare up at him, noticing for the first time a cleanly healed cut on his forearm. The puckered scar tissue shows white and fresh.

"Don't worry about getting back," I say.

He doesn't reply.

"I'm sure Frieda's parents will make sure you get home. You might even have a chance to ride in a cab."

He stares into the distance. A tear forms at the corner of his eye, falls onto his cheek. He doesn't say anything.

Frieda rolls into the kitchen. She's wearing jeans, a button-down shirt, and a frown. "Sally's not in my bedroom," she whispers. "I've looked all over and I can't find her!"

"I don't know where she is either," I say. "I left her in the room with the glass doors."

Her jaw drops. "The library? I just went past it. That's where the Tutankhamen Society is meeting."

I think about the incense. And the stone planter, as big as a bathtub. And the picture of the Sphinx.

"Oh," I say.

Somebody screams – a shrill piercing sound that goes on and on.

11

The Messenger of Anubis

The glass doors are open. All the lights are on in the library. Weird music is playing softly. We stare in from the hallway.

The room is full of well-dressed people. Women in hats, men in suits. They are all sitting around the marble table, except for one small man, with black hair and eyes to match, who is standing beside a flip chart; and one large woman, with purple hair and lips to match, who is sprawled back against the bookshelves with her hand covering her mouth.

She's the screamer. "In there!" Her purple-tipped finger points at the planter in the center of the table. Flower tops peep over the rim, and there's a dinky pine tree sticking out, like the mast of a small boat. Very decorative. I notice the picture writing on the sides of the planter. "Anubis!" she cries. "I saw him – as large as life!"

We studied Ancient Egypt in school last year, so I know that the picture writing is hieroglyphics, and the planter is really a sarcophagus – a kind of coffin.

"Really?" says the small man by the flip chart. His shoulder-length hair is long and thick and black. The rest of his body is short and thin and pale. "Really? There are records of divine visitation on the Rosetta stone," he says, in an accent from *Masterpiece Theater*. "And there is a group on the West Coast who claim the god Thoth as a regular communicant. Tell me what you saw just now!" He leans forward. His eyes are huge. His body vibrates with interest.

It might be a school assembly, but it might be a church service too. There's an atmosphere of mystery. The incense is part of it. So is the music – scales with missing notes, played on things that sound like pop bottles and tin cans.

"I tell you, I saw him!" says the purple lady. A frightened but, at the same time, tremendously excited look is on her face. Not the sort of look you see in an assembly – or, very often, in church, for that matter. "Quiet! Listen!"

Behind the music, even I can hear an irregular scratching noise. It seems to be coming from *inside* the sarcophagus.

The lights flicker. Thunder booms outside. Everyone jumps.

There's power here; I can feel it. The curtains are drawn, shutting us in. I can hear the rain beating against the windows.

Bird smiles next to me.

"Can you believe all this?" I whisper.

"Shew-ah," he says.

I'm trying to remember which god Anubis is. I think he's the one with the pointy ears and a long nose. But he's not real. He can't be real, can he? Ancient Egypt was five thousand years ago. We learned about it in history class, just before the Ancient Greeks. If Anubis is real, does that mean that Zeus and Athena are real too?

I'm carrying my uncertainty like a bag of rocks. There's another prolonged scratching sound, and a head appears above the rim of the sarcophagus. Like Anubis', this head has pointy ears and a long nose. Also, a pink tongue.

"There!" screams the purple woman.

The effect is electric. Gasps, screams. The purple woman points triumphantly. Another woman covers her face with her hands. The guest speaker stares as if he would swallow the apparition with his black eyes. A fat man at the far end of the table falls sideways in a faint. Good thing the carpets are soft.

Needless to say, I don't feel any of this excitement. The second I actually see the mystery being, and hear its voice, the atmosphere clears. The thunder is just thunder. My worry floats away. When the apparition speaks, I feel an overwhelming desire to giggle.

– Is it hot in here, or is it me? And what's with the smell? On Jupiter, we take our smells seriously. You could get in trouble for burning this stuff.

Frieda lets out a little squeal of delight. She rolls herself into the room. Bird and I follow. "Talkin' dog," says Bird. No one pays any attention to us.

"What did I tell you!" cries the purple-haired, purple-nailed, purple-lipped lady. Voices rise like bubbles in soda. "Help us, Professor Malchus!" the lady cries.

The little man in black takes charge. I guess he's the professor. He's got the right kind of voice, as deep and rich as a layer cake. "O dog-headed being! Apparition with Anubis' face! Relic of Ancient Empire! Speak to us!" he cries, his arms raised, his voice warm and quivering.

The assembly, or congregation, gives a collective moan of horror and excitement.

Sally whines.

– *Awoooooooo!* says Norbert, in a spooky squeaky voice. Filtered through Sally's whine, it sounds other-worldly. *Awoooooooo! Anubis to you too.*

"He speaks to us from across the centuries!" cries the professor.

– *That's me,* says Norbert. *Across the centuries, here in your home.*

"But you are not Anubis," says the professor. "Anubis has the body of a man."

– *Who?*

"Anubis, the god of the dead!"

– *Oh, I remember him! My uncle told me all about him. Umm . . . No. Anubis couldn't come today. He was busy, so he sent me.*

"Then, who are you?"

A long pause. The whole society is leaning forward, as if their life's dream has knocked on the door and asked to borrow a cup of sugar. I don't dare laugh.

– *You may call me . . . Norberto!*

I cover my mouth with my hand. The professor frowns.

"Norberto?" he says. "Norberto? I have spent my life learning about Ancient Egypt. I have read everything that has been written on the subject. And I have never heard of Norberto." He walks towards the table as if under a spell.

– *So what? Norberto has never heard of you. Awooooo!*

"Fascinating!" Professor Malchus reaches out to touch the sarcophagus. His hand trembles. "There's so much I want to know. So much I want to ask you."

The table moans in agreement.

– *Sure, sure. But first, Norberto – I mean, Anubis – has a message for you.*

"For me?" The professor chokes.

– *Well, actually, no. Not for you. I have a message for a . . . Mrs. Miller.*

"Gladys!" screams the purple lady. "It's for you!" She sounds like a kid sister answering the telephone.

A soft cry from our side of the table. Frieda's mom. She's sitting with her back to the door. I recognize her because of the tall rounded hat.

"Me?" she whispers. Frieda's mom all right. But she sure doesn't sound like she did a half hour ago.

Beside me, Frieda goes very still. She's not smiling now.

– *Yes, you.*

Before Norbert can say any more, Sally sneezes. And again.

– *Better get rid of the smoke. It's driving me crazy.*

"The incense is not traditional?" asks Professor Malchus.

– *No. Can't stand it. The music can go too.*

"But there are pictures. I've seen them, on tomb walls. The hieroglyphics are very clear. Do you mean that those braziers in the pictures aren't burning incense? That it's . . . something else?"

– *Marshmallows,* says Norbert shortly.

Professor Malchus shakes his head, as if he hasn't heard right.

Mrs. Miller picks up the brass vase with the burning sticks in it and rushes out of the room. Sally yawns. There's a collective in-drawing of breath.

I turn to Frieda. "Your mother's name is Gladys?" She nods.

Mrs. Miller returns without the brass vase. The weird music disappears too.

– *Much better,* says Norbert.

She bows towards him. A dramatic woman, six feet tall, robed in black. "Pardon our ignorance, Norberto. We didn't know."

– *That's okay. Don't grovel, Glinda. I hate groveling.*

"Sorry, Norberto. My name is Gladys, by the way. Not Glinda. Gladys Miller. I was Gladys Simons until I married Phil. Do you know Phil? He's a state representative."

– *I know ten thousand Phils,* says Norbert dismissively.

Sally gets up on her front paws and stares in our direction.

– Gladys Miller, this message is for you. Are you listening? Are you prepared to heed the messenger of Anubis?

"I am," says Gladys.

The doorbell rings.

– The message of Anubis is simple. Treasure your child.

"My . . . do you mean Frieda?" Mrs. Miller doesn't sound dramatic anymore; just puzzled.

– I mean Frieda. She is your greatest claim to fame. You are a mother. You and your Phil have the honor to be the parents of . . . Frieda.

"You're saying you know Frieda? Does Anubis know her?"

– All of us on the other side know Frieda, and esteem her highly. Her fame stretches around time the way an elastic stretches around a jar to keep the waxed paper on.

"Huh?"

– It's a line from a country and western song. Forget it, Glenda.

"Gladys."

– Whatever. Oh, and by the way, would you mind taking off that stupid hat?

Her eyes widen. "Frieda is back from Canada today . . . Norberto. I think she's. . . ." Mrs. Miller turns in her chair. Sees us all. "Oh, there you are," she says to Frieda.

Frieda doesn't say anything.

– Take off the hat! Do as I say, woman!

I open my mouth to burst out laughing, but at that moment a bolt of lightning flashes nearby. A crack of thunder rocks the house. The lights flicker. And I don't feel like laughing.

Frieda's mom has her hat off in a jiffy. Underneath, her hair is short and yellow.

– *Now, give your daughter a hug.*

The doorbell rings again, insistently. Gladys and Frieda stare at each other.

– *Don't be afraid of her,* says Norbert.

Frieda's eyes narrow. "Afraid?" she says. "Mother, are you . . . afraid of me?" Her mother looks away.

Thunder outside, very close. I hear Beatrice's voice from the front door. "You can't do that!" she says.

Professor Malchus moves closer to the sarcophagus. His hand is in his jacket pocket. He peers closely. "Oh, Norberto," he begins, in a low voice.

– *Do you mind, there, mop-head?* says Norbert. *A little privacy, hey? This is a single room.*

The professor mutters something inaudible.

– *What was that? Build what? Oh, the pyramids. Sure. My Uncle Nathan helped. You should hear him talk about Cheops. What a blowhard!*

"Cheops!" Unable to contain himself, the professor almost shouts the word. His eyes are huge and round. "You know about his . . . about the Great. . . ."

Before he finishes the question, a man and a woman enter the room. He's tired and old, and so are his clothes. She's sharp, and so are hers. Behind them walks a young man with muscles. His clothes are blue. All blue. He's a policeman. He stops by the double doors with his arms folded.

The woman's eyes are sharp enough to peel fruit. She stares at the professor, at Frieda's mom, at us kids. Her gaze makes me feel like a skinned apple.

The older man takes out a wallet and flips it open. "Sorry to interrupt your meeting, ladies and gentlemen," he says. "I'm Special Agent Libby, Customs and Excise. This is Lieutenant Aylmer, NYPD liaison. The man by the door is Officer Culverhouse."

No one says anything. Special Agent Libby flips the wallet closed, puts it back in his pocket, and smiles at the professor. "Hello, Earless," he says.

12

Earless

"Whom are you addressing, sir?" The professor's expression is exactly right: puzzled and apologetic.

Libby takes out a sheet of paper and reads from it: "Simon Peter Malchus, also known as Professor Malchus, Brother Malchus, Dr. Malchus, and, once, Detective Sergeant Malchus – tut-tut, impersonating a police officer." The special agent smiles broadly. "Known to intimates as Earless after a regrettable incident in his youth – a knife fight under the shadow of the Great Pyramid."

Frieda and I stare at each other. *Earless will be happy to see him.* I shiver, thinking back to the scene in the alley with Slouchy.

"Born Biddeford, Maine. Master's degree in Egyptology from NYU. Noted collector of art and artifacts. Dealer in same. Convicted smuggler." He stops. "Nice varied profile here, Earless."

"I'm sorry, sir, but I really don't see why you're here. My name is Malchus, that's true. Not a common name – but not unique. You've got me mixed up with this Peter Malchus. Some kind of a clerical error."

The special agent smiles. "Perhaps." Then, suddenly, he takes two strides forward and grabs the professor by the hair. "Do you mind?" he says, lifting his hand.

I gasp. Frieda gasps. The rest of the Tutankhamen Society gasps.

The professor has no outer ear. Just a little rim of cartilage. The side of his head is flat. He sighs. "I don't think that proves anything."

"No, Earless, it doesn't prove anything, but I think it's a good indicator, don't you? You happen to be missing most of one ear, and your name happens to be Malchus. And you happen to be addressing the Tutankhamen Society in a posh house here on the Upper West Side. You might even have mentioned your most recent acquisition. A good luck charm, supposedly representing the weeping Horus."

The professor sniffs disdainfully. "You may choose to call it a good luck charm, sir. The correct term is *Ushabti*."

Horus? Frieda's hand reaches up instinctively to touch her earrings.

Some members of the society are looking perturbed. Is the professor sweating? I can't tell. He sounds calm and cultured, like an advertisement for tonic water.

The sharp-eyed lieutenant takes over now. "Ladies and gentlemen, Malchus here really knows his Ancient Egypt.

He's a bit of a fanatic on the subject of the pyramids. But he's a fraud. He's not a real professor. He's an avid collector and a smuggler and a criminal, and we've been on his trail – and this Ushabti Horus – for months." She points at the sarcophagus. "Very nice piece. Middle Kingdom, Earless? Maybe Eighteenth Dynasty?"

The professor sniffs again. "As anyone here in the room could tell you, Lieutenant Aylmer, the Middle Kingdom ended long before the Eighteenth Dynasty," he says.

The lieutenant doesn't seem embarrassed – in fact she looks pleased – and then it occurs to me that she's got the professor to answer to the name Earless. And, you know, it's getting harder to think of him as the "professor" and easier to think of him as Earless.

Special Agent Libby tells us how the Ushabti moved from Egypt to New York. A complicated story. My favorite part was when it was carried through the streets of Antwerp by a schoolgirl who thought it was a box of chocolates. And talk about thorough: Libby even knows the schoolgirl's name. He tries to check his facts – "Then, by boat from Belgium to Canada, right, Earless?" – but the professor doesn't say anything. "And finally, today, to New York by plane. And we're executing a search and seizure warrant on the 37th Street gallery right now."

Earless looks up. Libby smiles at him. "Yes, if there's anything incriminating at Amphora Jones, we'll find it."

"Excuse me!" cries the fat man who fainted before. He's alert now. "Are you saying that New York galleries like Amphora Jones are dealing in stolen property? That Professor Malchus' Ushabti is not really his to sell?

"Do you have the Ushabti, sir?" Agent Libby asks eagerly. "Did you see it? We have every link in the chain of evidence, except proof of the artifact in Malchus' hands."

The fat man shakes his head. His jowls wobble. "He was going to show it to us when . . . Norberto interrupted."

The special agent frowns.

"I have a question," says the purple lady. "Before the police arrived, we all witnessed a truly strange encounter. A messenger of a god was in this room, sir."

The law enforcement agents look at one another.

"I just want to know if Professor Malchus thinks it was real, or if that, too, was a part of his scheme," she adds.

I understand what Lieutenant Aylmer meant about Earless being a fanatic. His eyes are round and dark, and as wide-open as bear traps. I feel I can't look away. The eyes seem to absorb the light, as if it can't get away either. Fanatic's eyes.

He has all our attention. "In my opinion, the encounter was real. We were fortunate. I never thought I would have the privilege of conversation with an immortal."

"Huh?" says Libby.

"The messenger of Anubis is in this room. He promised to tell me about the building of the pyramids, knowledge I would give anything – *anything* – to have."

The Tutankhamen Society nods collectively. They believe Earless. I'd be tempted to believe him myself, if I didn't know that the immortal he's talking about is a dog with an alien from Jupiter in its nose.

Agent Libby doesn't believe him. He blinks. "Sure, Earless," he says. "You can tell it all to the judge. Encounter with a god's messenger. Diminished capacity might be a good defence, at that."

"Norberto understands me," says Earless. "Norberto will direct me. My faith is sure."

And, at that precise moment, a gigantic peal of thunder rocks the house. The lights go out.

"Nobody move!" cries Libby from the middle of the darkness.

I don't move, but someone does. I hear a clatter and clash, and a squeaky voice saying – *Hey, beat it! Go on, now! Get him, Sally!*

The lights come on a few seconds later.

The police officer – Culverhouse – is still standing by the doors. Sally is on the floor, shaking herself.

Earless is gone.

The next quarter of an hour is very busy. Lieutenant Aylmer races after Earless. Special Agent Libby shouts alternately into a walkie-talkie and a cell phone. Officer Culverhouse, looking embarrassed, starts asking everyone their names and addresses, and writing down the information in a notebook. He even asks us.

"Cobourg?" he says to me. "Where's that?" I tell him.

He asks me to wait around. "Agent Libby may want to talk to you himself," he adds.

Bird's address is harder to pinpoint. He takes Culverhouse to a window and gestures.

"What'll we tell them?" I ask Frieda. She has her eyes shut, hugging the dog.

"About what?"

"You know. About the kidnapping. About Slouchy and Skinny and Veronica."

"Oh." She opens her eyes, frowns. "I don't know. I'm not thinking about that. I just can't get over what Norbert said. Do you think my mom is afraid of me? Is that why she doesn't pay any attention to me?"

"I don't know," I say.

The Tutankhamen Society is finally allowed to leave. Everyone looks upset on their way out the door. No one thanks Frieda's mom for a lovely time. Now it's only us and the law. Beatrice is making coffee in the kitchen. Mrs. Miller shudders when she notices Frieda playing with Sally.

"You know, I've never really liked dogs," she says.

"Where'd this one come from?" asks Agent Libby.

"I don't know. I'm . . . afraid to ask."

"But it is yours, isn't it?"

"I . . ." Sally races around Frieda's wheelchair like an out-of-control satellite, whirling off from under the marble table, then coming back and racing around the other way.

"Isn't it your dog, ma'am?"

Sally jumps up on her hind legs to put her front paws on the arms of Frieda's chair. For a second she looks like something out of a book on Ancient Egypt. It's her ears, so wide and pointed, and her long body. For a second she looks like a dog-headed human. Like – Anubis.

Mrs. Miller covers her eyes. And nods.

"Sure it is," says Frieda, grabbing Sally by both ears and wagging her head up and down. Sally slips back onto all fours. "Aren't you, sweetie?" Sally yawns.

Libby's walkie-talkie crackles. He answers it at once. "Did you get him?" he asks.

Apparently not. The special agent sighs. The pinches and folds of his cheeks look like wrinkles in a bedsheet.

Frieda takes us to her room. It's a big one, with two windows. Neat as a pin. No papers or unlabeled computer discs lying around. No sign of her dirty clothes. No chairs, not even in front of the desk. Bird goes over to the nearer window and stares out. I sit on the tightly made-up bed.

"What'll I tell the police?" I say. "They're going to ask how I came here. It's all going to come out. What'll I say, Frieda? What'll we both say?"

"I don't know." She doesn't look at me. She has eyes only for Sally, curled up beside me on the bed. Norbert coughs.

– *You might just tell the truth,* he says.

Bird looks around, smiles, then goes back to the window.

"But . . . I promised the slouchy guy I wouldn't tell. I promised."

Norbert snorts.

– *I just want to know if this is the same boy who promised his mother that he would tidy his room every day. "Do you promise, Alan?" she asked, and you said, "Yes, Mom, I promise."*

I don't say anything.

– *The same boy who promised a certain girl in Cobourg . . . now, what was her name?*

"Hey, shut up!" I say.

– *Promises, promises,* says Norbert.

Frieda looks over. She's blushing. I'm blushing too.

Sally yawns. It looks like she's sticking out her tongue at me.

I join Bird at the window. Frieda rolls herself over to the bed to stroke Sally. "You're my dog, now. Do you hear, Sally?"

The dog whines.

"We'll have to take you to the vet's," she says. "And get you a proper collar. This one is too rough."

Sally gets down from the bed and whines again.

"Oh, dear. Maybe she has to go to the bathroom," Frieda says.

We all stare at the dog.

– *She's hungry,* says Norbert. *And thirsty.*

"You sure she doesn't want to go outside?" I ask. My friend Miranda – that's the certain girl Norbert was talking about – has a dog named Gracie who has to go outside so often that her doggie door never shuts. Miranda's dad is a kind of scientist; he wonders if it's theoretically possible for Gracie, on her way back inside, to collide with herself going out again.

– *No, she's fine,* says Norbert. *That's why she was in the bathtub thing. She's hungry, I tell you.*

"What?" says Frieda. "Sally pooped in my mother's prize sarcophagus?"

– *Hey, I didn't choose the spot. It was Sally's idea.*

"Norbert!" I say.

– *Don't look at me. I'm civilized. I've got indoor plumbing here.*

Sally is still whining.

"Food's in the kitchen," says Bird, sensibly.

13

Papers

Sally likes leftover stew, we discover. Also, cheese biscuits and ladyfingers and bread crusts. And peanut butter. And raw broccoli. Not a picky eater. I want to offer her some weird smelly meat spread we find in the fridge, but Frieda says no.

– *Thank you,* says Norbert.

Through the open door of the kitchen we hear Mrs. Miller's voice. She's in the library with Special Agent Libby.

"It's hard to believe," she says. "Professor Malchus is such a gentleman. And so knowledgeable. We were all looking forward to seeing his new Ushabti. He was convinced it had a pyramid connection."

"So he did have it with him. Did he show you?"

"We didn't get that far," she said. "He described it for us. Horus – he's the hawk-faced Sky god, you know – is shown weeping. A very rare form."

"Hawkface," I say out loud. "Remember, Frieda?"

Frieda looks at me. It's the look my friend Victor gives me during math class. *Well, duh,* says the look.

– *You know, he left something in the sarcophagus,* says Norbert. *He dropped it in when the police came in the room, and then tried to get it back on his way out. He spoke to me very nicely. I think he really believes in Norberto.*

"What happened when he tried to get it back?" I ask.

– *Sally bit him.*

The dog whines.

– *Yes, yes,* says Norbert. *But you think that about everything.*

"What?" I ask.

– *Oh, nothing. She says it smelled funny. Don't ask me. She thinks everything smells funny. She's a dog, for heaven's sake.*

The agent is asking Mrs. Miller about Sally. "This messenger, now. There are a number of conflicting statements. Did you see the, um, creature?"

"Yes, sir."

"A dog? Now, I saw a dog here myself. A family dog, I assume. Is she yours, ma'am?"

"She's . . . with my daughter."

"Several statements claim that the dog was speaking to *you*, ma'am. To you directly, I mean. Did you hear it?"

Mrs. Miller clears her throat. "Oh, yes. Yes, I heard it plainly."

"Barking? Growling?"

Mrs. Miller doesn't say anything.

I get an idea. "The sarcophagus," I whisper to Frieda.

She's already rolling herself into the library. Sally looks up at me from the floor. *Well, duh*. Victor, Frieda, now Sally – everyone seems to look at me the same way.

"Do you think this Horus thing is in the sarcophagus?" I ask Bird.

"Shew-ah," he says. "But I don't want to fish it out."

We follow Frieda and Sally into the library.

Special Agent Libby doesn't have to do the dirty work himself, of course. Officer Culverhouse roots around in the sarcophagus. He uses tongs.

"Got something else!" The officer holds up another small dirt-covered lump. It's about as thick as my thumb, and not much longer. I'm all set to say yuck again, but on closer inspection I can see that it's a small statue – about three thousand years older than the first dirt-covered lump he fished out.

So that's an Ushabti.

"Careful," says the special agent. It's an automatic response. He sounds like your parents do when you're walking near the edge of a cliff.

Culverhouse places the Ushabti in a clear plastic bag, sticks a tag on it, and goes to wash his hands.

Libby frowns down at Frieda. "You are a very smart young lady," he says. "How did you know that was here?"

"Norberto told her!" cries Mrs. Miller, clapping her hand over her mouth, like teenagers do on TV commercials when they're worried about bad breath.

"There there," says the special agent. He takes her by the hand and leads her to a chair. "You're all upset, ma'am. You should rest a bit. I'm afraid this has all been a shock to you."

Sally jumps up on her hind legs to sniff energetically at the bundle on the table. Libby pushes it away from her. "Down, boy," he says.

"It's a girl dog," says Frieda. "Her name is Sally."

"I thought it was Norberto," he says.

I can't help noticing the way Mrs. Miller keeps staring at her daughter. When we first came into the house, she didn't pay any attention to her at all. Now she'll look away for a bit, then sneak a peek out of the corner of her eye.

"What's that smell?" says Culverhouse, when he comes back from washing his hands.

Sally whines.

"No, no," says Culverhouse. "I got a dog at home; I know that smell. This is like tar."

"Oh, that." Libby explains. "That's creosote. The Ushabti would probably have been wrapped in waterproof paper for transport overseas. The smell lingers."

Waterproof paper. I find myself staring at Sally. She cocks her head on one side. I remember the scene in the alley – Norbert telling her to *put it down, Sally. It stinks.* I remember reaching down to pick up the paper and put it in my . . .

– *Pocket.* Did I say that, or did Norbert? I reach into my pocket and pull out the piece of brown paper. It still stinks.

"Where'd you get that?" asks Libby.

I don't know what to say.

He stares at me. "Young man, we're going to have a talk," he says.

The dog puts her head in Frieda's lap. Mrs. Miller shudders.

14

You Are the Boy

Events are moving too fast for me. I feel like I'm in a weird dream. In this dream I'm standing still, and everything else in the world is whirling past. I grasp at objects I recognize but my hand closes around smoke, or empty air, or something totally unexpected. I reach for a tennis racket and get a spoon. I hear a friend's voice, but by the time I turn around I'm staring into the mouth of an angry lion. I try to take my father's hand and find myself clutching a stone.

What is happening to me? Why didn't Dad meet me at the airport? How did I come to be mixed up with a rich girl, a talking dog, and a smelly package? Not to mention bad guys, with names like Earless and Slouchy and Hawkface – no, Hawkface is a god. What does it all mean?

Maybe it *is* a weird dream. But it feels awfully real, and it's lasting all day long.

Anyway, when Special Agent Libby says hello and asks

me how I am, I say the first thing that comes into my head. "Confused," I say.

We're in the den. There's a grand piano at one end of the room and a couch at the other. Family photographs smile down from the walls. Flowers hold their heads up straight and tall in vases. The agent and I are sitting side by side on the couch.

"First trip to New York?" he asks. I nod. "Well, that explains it," he says. "It's a confusing town."

He rubs his face with his hand, kneading it hard, like pie crust. "I'm confused, and I've lived here all my life," he says. "Take this afternoon. I've been working on Earless for the past six months. I've got a pipeline into his organization. I've been following this Ushabti every step of the way, waiting for it to come to Earless himself. I had everything I needed to get him this afternoon – and you saw what happened."

"Too bad," I say.

He shakes his head. "You don't know the half of it. My people are searching through his gallery right now. I say 'his,' but there's nothing there that links up to Earless. The gallery isn't even in his name. I want him behind bars, and for that I need proof."

Of course, he also needs to have Earless himself, who is missing, but I don't point this out. "Sorry," I say.

He shrugs. "Not your fault."

He's an okay guy. He asks a bunch of easy questions in a really friendly tone of voice – where I live, how old I am, do I like baseball. I start to relax, maybe because he likes baseball too. "I went to last night's game with the Blue Jays," he says. "Got Williams' autograph – for my son," he adds. "He's about your age."

"Wow," I say.

"Would you like to see it? It's right here." He reaches into his inside jacket pocket.

Sally wanders into the room. I smile and beckon, but she jumps onto the couch next to the agent. He frowns. I don't think he likes dogs.

"Come here, Norb – I mean, Sally," I say. "C'mere, girl."

– *No,* says Norbert.

Startled by the strange squeaky voice, Libby jerks his hand out of his pocket. A photograph falls out, and lands on the glass-topped table right in front of me, as if placed by an unseen hand for my personal inspection. Nothing to do with baseball. This is a picture of Slouchy and Skinny sitting at a restaurant.

"I . . . I . . ." I stare and swallow. My hand, as if acting on its own impulse, nothing to do with my brain at all, reaches towards the photograph. "Who are they?" I ask. My voice comes from a long way off. It sounds like someone else's.

Libby stares at the dog, shakes his head, and then comes back to me. "These jokers? They're a couple of guys Earless uses here in New York. One of them works at La Guardia Airport. They're related – cousins, I think. Why? Do you . . . do you mean you recognize them? You've seen them?"

I nod.

"It's something to do with that piece of brown paper in your pocket, isn't it?"

I nod again.

"Where and when did you see them?"

I don't say anything.

"Come on, son."

I swallow. "This morning," I say. "I saw them both this morning."

Oh, no. I've said it now. I'm scared, but I can't take it back. The whole thing is going to come out. You can lie down and take deep breaths and fool yourself into thinking you're not going to throw up, until the moment comes when you know you are. No good telling yourself it's the right thing to do. No good telling yourself the police are the good guys.

Seeing Slouchy in the picture brings all my fear to the surface. I'm scared of what he'll do to me.

Sally licks my hand, and trots out of the room.

The story only takes a few minutes to tell. About halfway through, the special agent stops me, goes to the door, and calls Culverhouse. Then he has me start at the beginning and tell it again, with Culverhouse taking notes. After I'm done, they go over and over certain parts of it. Am I sure they said Earless will be happy to see him? What time was that? What exactly did they say? Am I sure?

"I'm sure," I say, "and there's another person involved too. A woman." I tell them about Veronica. The agent nods, but he doesn't seem as interested in her. "She's the attendant," I say. "On the airplane."

"Yeah, yeah," he says. He tells me to forget about her.

Frieda and Bird are called into the room and asked to confirm my story. Sally comes too. Frieda strokes the dog absently. Mrs. Miller stands in the doorway while Frieda speaks. She's staring at her daughter as if she's seeing a whole new person. When Frieda gets to the part where the truck drives away with us in it, Culverhouse clucks his teeth sympathetically. Mrs. Miller turns away. Frieda scratches behind Sally's ears.

Libby wants to hear one more time about the bundle inside the wheelchair. "Andrews and Jones both knew about it?" he asks. Andrews is Slouchy's real name. Jones is the skinny government guy, and he owns the Amphora Jones gallery – at least, his name is on the deed.

"They both knew," I say for the third time. "And Veronica unwrapped it. She wanted to take it to Earless herself, but the slouchy guy – Andrews – said no."

Libby nods to himself.

"Later, Sally found part of the wrapping," says Frieda. "Didn't you, sweetie!"

"And it smelled like creosote," I say.

The special agent is massaging his face again. He looks hopeful. I feel for him. I know how hard hope can be.

Here's a strange thing. After I talk to the C & E – that's what Customs and Excise call themselves – I feel better. You'd think I'd be worried. I've broken a promise. I've told, after I said I wouldn't. If Slouchy finds me, who knows what horrible thing he'll do.

Maybe I should feel scared. But I don't. I don't feel scared at all. I feel relieved. It's like I've been walking around with a stomach-ache. Now that I've thrown up, I feel better.

"I want to phone my dad," I say.

A half hour later I'm sitting in the kitchen with milk and cookies, listening for the phone. I'm hoping my dad will call back. His secretary said he would. I told her where I was, and gave her the Millers' number, and she said my dad would be sure to call back. She said that – *I'm sure he will* – in a voice I've heard my mom use, meaning *he should, but he might not get around to it.*

The secretary sounded surprised that I was in New York. "You sure you're not calling from Canada?" she asks.

Special Agent Libby is waiting for a call too. He's pacing up and down the kitchen, folding phone in one hand, cookie in the other.

Bleep!!

A ring, but not the one I want. "Yes?" says Libby. Crumbs spray out of his mouth. He ignores them. "Where is she?" he asks. "Why hasn't she called?" He stops moving and listens. "Say that again," he says. A late lightning flash lights up the sky outside; the flash is reflected in his eyes. "That's at La Guardia? Are you sure?"

He takes a small pad of paper from his inside jacket pocket – not the pocket with the photographs; the other one – and writes down some numbers. "Got it," he says.

"Anything else?" He's pressing the phone against his ear. Here's the hope again, riding across his face like a hero on a white horse. "Okay," he says. "Let's go. Clear it up the line. Use my authority. I want units in position in . . ." he looks at his watch ". . . in forty minutes. I'll get there with the boy as soon as I can."

He comes over to where I'm sitting, and bends down so his eyes are on a level with mine.

"I'm the boy, aren't I?" I say. "The boy you were just talking about on the phone."

He nods. "Jones' car is sitting in the airport parking lot. We need someone who saw it in the alley with the kidnappers' truck."

"Me?"

The special agent points to Bird. "He didn't see the car. You did."

"So I'm the boy?"

"You are the boy."

"Hey!" says Frieda.

15

Don't Know Yet

"What about me?" says Frieda.

Libby puts away his telephone. He looks almost naked without it. "What about you, Miss Miller?" I'm the boy. She's Miss Miller.

"Why can't I go?"

"Do you want to go, um, dear?" asks Frieda's mother. The last word sounds odd on her tongue, as though she isn't used to it.

"If Alan goes, I should go too. Two witnesses are better than one. I'm older than Alan, and I have a better memory."

Go instead of me, I think to myself. But I don't say it.

"But, Miss Miller, you're . . . well, you're . . ."

"A girl?"

"No. I mean, you are a girl, of course. But . . ." The agent is having trouble saying what he means.

"Maybe you'd better let the man decide," says Mrs. Miller.

"He's saying I can't go because I'm a girl," says Frieda.

"No, no, that's not it at all," he hastens to say. "It's . . . oh, dear."

She swivels her chair to face me. "Alan, what kind of car does the skinny guy drive?" she asks.

I think back. "It's medium-sized," I say. "Not too big. And not . . . what's the word?"

"Small?" says Bird.

"No no. Not all one color."

"Two-toned, yes," says Frieda. "How many doors?"

I open my mouth. "Doors?"

She smiles sympathetically. She doesn't want to make me look like an idiot. "Doors," she says. "The things with hinges and handles that people use to get in and out of cars."

Maybe she doesn't care what I look like, at that.

"I don't know," I say. "I only saw one."

Norbert snickers. I know it's Norbert. So does Frieda. She puts her hand on the dog's muzzle. "Shhh," she whispers.

The special agent is staring at me. I know that look. He's disappointed. My math teacher looks that way all the time. "Sorry," I say.

"It's a late-model Buick Regal hardtop," she says crisply. "Two-toned in blue. Light blue body, dark blue top."

"I didn't know you were interested in automobiles, dear," says her mother.

"Four doors," she goes on. "And one of those pathetic tassels tied to the aerial."

Libby is still staring at me. "I remember the tassel," I say.

So Frieda gets to come to the airport too. With her is her mom, hesitant but determined. And Sally. The special agent doesn't want to take the dog, but Frieda insists. "You'll see," she says. "There's more to this dog than you think there is."

"That's true," says Mrs. Miller.

"That's true," I say.

– *That is true,* says Norbert.

We're all in the Millers' front hall. Libby frowns, shakes his head, opens the door.

"What about my dad?" I say. "He's going to call here." If he remembers. But I don't say that. "I don't want to miss his call. I've missed him all day."

"Beatrice will tell him where you are," says Frieda.

Beatrice is standing next to me, holding the front door open. She pats my arm.

"He was supposed to meet me at the airport this morning," I say.

"But the plane was early," says Beatrice. "Don't worry, little one. I will wait for your call. A boy should be with his *padre*."

We're cramped in the unmarked C & E car. I'm in the front, between Special Agent Libby and Officer Culverhouse. Frieda and her mom and Sally are in the back. The storm is over, and the pavements are steaming in the misty sunshine. Everyone but me and Sally is wearing sunglasses. Frieda's new pair look like her old ones. Mrs. Miller's have pale yellow rims, to match her topcoat.

Bird is in the back too. Driving past Central Park, the special agent asks him where he thinks he's going.

"Airport," says Bird.

"Why?"

"Don't know yet," says Bird.

"Where's your wagon?" Frieda asks.

"Got what I need from it," he says. He reaches into a capacious pocket and brings out a woven leather leash. "For you and your talkin' dog. Happy Wishday."

"Oh, Bird. I can't take it."

"You got to – it's the law."

Frieda weighs it in her hand. "Then, thank you," she says. "Thank you very much."

"Shew-ah."

"But how do you know that this is all you need?"

"I just know."

There's a hands-free phone in the car. A female voice on the other end of the phone wonders where we are and how long it will take us to get to La Guardia. Lieutenant Aylmer's voice. "Ten minutes," Libby tells her.

The East River is behind us now. We're in Queens. Culverhouse drives fast, headlights flashing. Cars ahead of us pull out of the way.

"I'll meet you at the west entrance," says Lieutenant Aylmer. "They've blocked off a large section of the east side for a movie they're shooting."

"Those signs we saw this morning," I say to Frieda. "Remember?"

"Of course I remember," she says. "We passed a crew setting up tracks for the camera."

"We did?"

On an impulse, Mrs. Miller stretches her arm across her daughter's body. "Can I?" she asks, and strokes Sally behind the ears.

"I didn't know you liked dogs," says Frieda.

Traffic jam. Libby swears, and reaches under his seat for a blue light that clips onto the roof of the car. When the siren starts to wail, it's not quite like on TV. It's louder, for one thing.

Sally lets out a startled yelp and scrambles over Frieda's lap and onto Bird's. She's on her feet, trembling, taking up most of the backseat.

The car pulls left, across the double yellow line. Lights flashing, motor revving, we're barreling along in the wrong lane. Oncoming cars are leaping out of our way.

– *Down!* calls Norbert. I can't help it, I duck. So does Culverhouse. *Not you, Dingwall. Sally, down, girl!*

"Who's that?" asks Libby. "That you, Frieda?"

– *Sit!* says Norbert. I am sitting and, a moment later, so is Sally.

By now we're roaring into the airport. We park at the near end of the terminal, behind the cab rank. Before we can even get out of the car, Lieutenant Aylmer comes running over. She sticks her head in the window.

"You made good time, sir. We've set up a command post inside."

"Personnel?"

"The terminal is crawling with cops and C & E agents. We're like fleas on a dog here."

– *Hey!* says a squeaky voice from the backseat.

"Shh," says Frieda.

Libby asks about Earless. Lieutenant Aylmer shakes her head.

We all get out of the car. Mrs. Miller helps Frieda into her chair, bending to swing her daughter's legs into position. Sally licks Mrs. Miller's hand. She gives a little shriek, then composes herself.

"I'm trying," she says. I don't know who she's talking to. "I am trying. I'm not afraid."

Aylmer steps back to let Libby out of the car. "You said you'd bring the boy, sir. Why's everyone else here?"

"Extra witnesses," Libby says shortly. "The girl's got a good memory. Boy's is like a sieve." He says this last bit in a low voice, but I hear it. Ah, well.

"I understand the car is in lot P-3," says Aylmer.

"Isn't that where it was parked this morning?" I ask.

"No," says Frieda. "It was across from the west taxi rank. Under the overhang."

"Oh, yeah," I say.

"See what I mean," Libby whispers.

Aylmer nods. "But the girl is. . . ." She doesn't finish.

"Yes, I know," he says.

The smell of plane exhaust makes this underground parking lot a bit more exciting than usual, but it's still a big gray grimy noisy low-ceilinged shed full of cars. P-3 is on the third level below ground. When we get there, the car is easy to spot. "There it is," I say, pleased with myself for beating Frieda to the punch.

"No," she says. "It's too small."

"But it's got a tassel on the aerial."

"So does that one there," she says, pointing to a red minivan. "And that one too." She points to a sports car, whose all-black windows are covered in stencils of bull dogs and bikinis. The licence plate says BAD DUDE. I wonder why he needs a tassel. You'd think he'd know which car was his.

Frieda wheels herself down one row of cars and up another one. Her mom walks beside us. Aylmer follows at a distance. She's in charge of us now. Libby and Culverhouse are busy inside the airport.

"There it is." Frieda sounds sure of herself. Blue and blue, like she said. It's parked carelessly between a Jeep with wooden siding and a black luxury sedan. Sally starts sniffing around the luxury car. I suppose it must have run over something especially smelly.

"Could be the right car," I say. "But there's no tassel."

Aylmer ignores me. Her sharp eyes glint. "Good for you," she tells Frieda. "You've tied the car to the kidnap scene. That's another charge on the slate against Jones. We have a forensics team standing by." She takes out a phone and gives some orders.

"You mean you knew all along," I say.

"Our pipeline was in the car," says Aylmer. "You guys are confirmation."

She punches a number into her cell phone and walks a short way off to talk.

It's 4:30 by my watch. I have a sudden clear picture of my dad, checking his watch as he makes a phone call. He always does that. The picture is so vivid, I can count the creases in Dad's summer suit, smell the aftershave he wears.

"What's wrong, Alan?" asks Frieda. She rolls herself over to where I'm standing, and puts her hand on my arm.

"Nothing," I say.

"For a second there you looked like you were going to burst into tears."

"Me?"

When I was a toddler I used to like to shave with my dad, early in the mornings. He'd sit me on the bathroom vanity and put foam on my cheeks, and give me a razor of my own without a blade in it, and after we'd wiped our faces clean he'd splash his aftershave on us both. I felt as grown up as you can feel, when you're still too young to go to school.

16

No One Belongs Here

"What the hell are you guys doing?" asks Aylmer. She glares at a fat sweaty woman and a thin dry man in zippered jumpsuits and plastic gloves and masks. The forensics team.

"We're doing what we're told," says the fat woman. The name stitched on her jumpsuit is MARIA. "Like always."

"Always," says the thin man, echoing his partner, nodding his head like a puppet. I can't read the name on his jumpsuit.

"Who told you to work on *that* car?" asks Aylmer in exasperation. The black luxury sedan is now covered in white powder and masking tape. "It's the wrong one, dammit!"

"You told us to start on the black car," says Maria. "Didn't you? Sounded like you."

"Like you," says the man.

"So Wolfgang and I got out our baggies and magic dust, and went to work."

"To work," says the thin dry man. He's got a reedy voice to match his body. He doesn't look or act like someone named Wolfgang. I wonder if his parents are disappointed. Call a baby Wolfgang and you're aiming high.

"Get away from the black car!" shouts Aylmer. "This blue one is the one we're interested in. I told you that an hour ago!"

"Okay," says Maria. She mops her streaming forehead with a handkerchief. "Whatever you say. This one, that one. Go here, go there. You're the boss."

"The boss," repeats Wolfgang.

"Pretty good fingerprints here on the black one," she says. "This driver's side door handle's got a couple of beauts. Full thumb and forefinger. Perfect. Eh, Wolfgang? You got pictures, right?"

"Pictures, right," says Wolfgang.

"Fingerprints always take well in this stuff. Funny, you don't notice the smell 'til you get close to it. Strong smelling stuff, this creosote."

"Creosote," says Wolfgang.

"Hold it," says Aylmer.

Police dogs are trained to sniff out contraband, and to ignore everything that isn't contraband. And creosote isn't contraband. The three police officers on K-9 detail shake their heads over the assignment. Their dogs will not follow a creosote trail.

"What am I supposed to do?" Agent Libby is back from

the command post. His forehead is ridged with frown wrinkles. His voice echoes around the underground parking lot. "I want a dog who can follow a scent. Do I have to fly in a bloodhound?" Then he catches sight of Sally.

Ten minutes and several phone calls later, we leave lot P-3 under police escort. Sally leads the way in her new leash, tracking confidently into the elevator and up three floors to the arrivals level. "I told you there was more to her than you'd think," says Frieda proudly. She's holding the other end of the leash. Sally won't follow a scent for anyone else.

Over the loudspeaker comes a voice speaking English. That's all I can tell. I have no idea what it's saying. Bird looks up, shakes his head, and keeps walking.

Earless – if it is Earless we're following, and not some poor guy with creosote on his hands from waterproofing his back fence – believes in exercise. He didn't take any of the moving sidewalks. The escort is spread out around us. Libby and Aylmer are beside us in a golf cart, the kind they usually use for pulling baggage wagons. Bird and I take turns pushing Frieda. She can't push herself and hang on to the leash. Mrs. Miller tried to keep up with us for a while, but she's on the back of the golf cart now, holding her side. Agent Libby is on the phone.

Signs are up, with arrows pointing. CLOSED TO PUBLIC. MOVIE EXTRAS THIS WAY. There's a policeman on guard. He's a fat guy, with a gut full of pretzels. He's eating one now. His mouth is open. Yuck. He waves us in without looking at anyone's credentials. Maybe he thinks we're part of the movie.

We come to a row of trailers. Sally is at the end of her leash, sniffing strongly. Taped to the door of the nearest trailer is a piece of paper. WARDROBE, it says.

The door opens suddenly and a cloud of smoke billows out. A woman follows the cloud. She's smoking a cigarette and carrying a garment bag.

She stops at the sight of us. "Police?" she asks. "If it's about that missing uniform, I don't know anything. They were all here this morning. Geez, does that dumb assistant director have the police running his errands now?" The cigarette in her mouth bobs around as she speaks. The rest of her stays still.

"Have you seen anyone who didn't belong here?" asks Libby.

The woman laughs, but she's not amused. Ash drops off her cigarette. "This project is ten days behind schedule and twenty million over budget," she says. "No one belongs here."

There's an announcement over the loudspeaker. I haven't been able to understand any of the other announcements at all, but this one comes through clear as a bell. "Passenger named Bird, report to TICKET INFORMATION. Passenger named Bird."

Bird is pushing the wheelchair now. He nods to himself. He's not surprised. It's like he's been waiting for his name to be called.

"Got to go," he says. "Bye, Frieda. Bye, Talkin' Dog. Bye, Alan."

He hands the wheelchair over to me. Then he takes off his wraparound sunglasses, folds them up, and hooks them onto the top of my soccer shirt. The dark glasses dangle, partially obscuring the donut picture. Do I feel not uncool? Actually, I feel more self-conscious than anything else. I turn to say thank you, but at that moment a crowd of people descends, smelling of gunpowder and cigarettes and talking at the top of their voices. They seem happy despite what look like dreadful wounds. Most of their costumes have bloodstains on the front. And bullet holes. They cluster around the front of the wardrobe trailer. The smoking lady asks them to let her past. They pay no attention to her. A man with a wispy beard pushes a trio of huge lights on a stand. He asks the crowd to let him through. They pay no attention to him.

Sally, who has been casting around for the true scent, lifts her head. Next thing I know, she's off in a new direction. I call over my shoulder to the police escort. Frieda hangs on to the leash. I push. After a moment the noise of the crowd recedes. The dog quests confidently – left turn, straight, right turn. We come to a set of glass doors that close and lock behind us. Now we're back in the public part of the airport. Moving sidewalks, passengers in a hurry. Sally urges us on. I look over my shoulder. I can't see the escort.

17

Elephant in Your Bedroom

Sally hurries forward, tongue out, straining hard against the leash. Frieda hangs on grimly. I practically have to run to keep up. The scene could be out of a Northern wilderness adventure story by Jack London or Farley Mowat, only our sled team is not in a blinding snowstorm in the middle of a six-month night. We are, in fact, in a crowded airport on a pleasant afternoon in early summer, and the dogsled is a wheelchair. Unlike the arctic travelers, I don't trust the dog. I'm afraid that Sally will pull us into real trouble. The very last thing we want is to meet Earless without our police escort.

"Stop, Sally!" I call. No use. I try to slow down the wheelchair with my body weight by grabbing the handles, but our gallant sled dog is more than a match for my weight. The sled slips out of my hands, and I stumble. I straighten up and trot after it. "Can you get her to slow down, Frieda?" I shout.

"Where's my mom?" she calls back. "Is she still here?"

"Or you could just let go!"

She doesn't hear me. "I won't let go!" she says.

Great.

Now, don't get the impression that we're tearing through the terminal at warp speed. Sally's pulling a chair and a kid – two kids, when I succeed in hanging on. But we are covering ground. Some of the people we pass tell us to watch where we're going.

There's an announcement about a plane arriving from Maui . . . or Malawi . . . or maybe the announcer is calling Howie. I can't tell. No one seems to care.

"Hey, Norbert!" I cry. He hasn't said much since we got to the airport. "Help! What is Sally doing?"

– She's following her nose. Very strong impulse for dogs and humans. Remember the five cheese pizza last year?

Sally is panting, but still full of energy. We turn down a corridor, away from the crowds of people.

– Oh, dear. The smell is getting stronger. I may have to open another cocoa air freshener packet in here. I hate those things. They don't even smell like real cocoa.

"Come on, Norbert," Frieda asks. "Can't you help at all?"

– Too late. Good luck now, you two.

"But. . . ."

Sally drags us away from the stream of people, down a narrow corridor. She stops in front of a dark blue door marked EMPLOYEES ONLY. It looks familiar.

"Wait a minute," says Frieda. Sally is whining and jumping up, and scratching at the woodwork. The door opens inwards.

"Earless? Is that you? It's me, Andrews."

A voice from a nightmare, but even before the words are out, I know we're in trouble. The smell of Slouchy's cologne travels faster than sound.

Slouchy grabs Sally by the collar, pulling her inside. Frieda follows on the other end of the leash, and I follow Frieda. And there we all are, in a small blue room with a table in the middle. The searching room beside baggage claims. No wonder it looks familiar.

Slouchy is not alone in the blue room. Skinny is there too, in his uniform, and so is Veronica, in hers. If Special Agent Libby were there, I'd point to Veronica and say, "See, I told you about her."

Veronica looks honestly worried when she sees us. "You two!" she says. "And alone! What are you doing here?"

I don't know what to do. I point to Sally. "It's her fault," I say.

Sally has her head cocked to one side. My friend Victor's dog does this when it brings a dead chipmunk into the house. Sally is proud of herself.

"Stupid animal," says Slouchy. "Bit me this morning. I don't know where I'd ever see a stupider animal."

– *You could look in a mirror,* says Norbert.

He frowns. His red hair comes down over his black eyebrows. "Who said that?" He stares at the dog, and then Frieda. "You say that, girlie?" Frieda shakes her head.

I'm so scared. This is exactly what I was hoping wouldn't happen.

"It was the dog's voice," says Skinny in his raspy way. "The dog there."

"Shut up!" snaps Slouchy. You know, I can see a family resemblance. Both men have close-set eyes, and short eyebrows. I can believe they're cousins. "That's crazy talk."

"Earless was telling me about a human dog before you got here," says Skinny. "It had a squeaky voice – just like this one."

"Well, Earless is crazy," says Slouchy. "Him and his pyramids! That's all he ever talks about. He cares more about those stupid mounds than anything else in the world."

When Skinny swallows, his big Adam's apple bobs up and down in his thin neck.

"Now, getting back to you two kids," says Slouchy.

Am I crying? I'm pretty close. Don't want to think about crying. Crying is not going to make things better.

Slouchy bends down between Frieda and me. He's got one hand on Frieda's wheelchair, and the other arm on my shoulder. He talks quietly. Gosh, is he scary. "We have to know how you got here. Did you talk? Did you talk to the police?" he asks.

I don't move. I'm too scared.

"Come on. Did you say anything? Did you tell anyone? What did you talk about?"

Frieda starts to stutter. "Tut - tut - tut . . ." she says.

"What was that?" His voice is smooth and warm, like a silk blanket. So why do I feel like shivering? "Come on, now, just tell me what you talked about."

"Tut - tut - tut . . ."

He turns to me. "What's she trying to say?"

I search my mind for inspiration. Like searching the fridge on Wednesday, the day before Mom goes shopping. I don't find anything useful at all.

"Tutankhamen," says Frieda at last.

"Tutankhamen?" Slouchy spits it out like a swear word. Then he says a whole bunch of swear words – including some I've never heard before. He straightens up. "That proves it!" he says. "They know. Earless was at the Tutankhamen Society this afternoon, eh, Jones?"

"That's where he saw the talking dog," says Skinny.

"These snotty kids must know about the whatchamacallit. The Ushabti. You know, don't you?" Slouchy says to Frieda. "You know, don't you, you crippled brat!"

He's strong. With one freckled hairy hand he picks Frieda out of the chair by the shirt collar. She swings an arm at him, trying to slap him again, maybe, but he pushes her against the wall. Her jeans ride up, exposing bulbous bumpy ankles. Her feet twist inwards.

I'm shocked. Not at Frieda's feet. I'm shocked that this should be happening to her.

Veronica frowns, but doesn't do anything to stop Slouchy. She reaches into the outside pocket of her blue flight attendant jacket, and keeps her hand there.

Slouchy keeps one hand on Frieda's shoulder, holding her up. "You know about the Horus statue, don't you? Bringing it into Canada from Europe, and then smuggling it across the American border inside your wheelchair. About my cousin here, the tame government man."

"Tame?" says Skinny. "Who's tame? It was my idea. And Earless put the gallery in my name."

"Yeah, well, he hired me first."

They're telling us all about it. I don't want to know, but they're telling us.

"You know about Amphora Jones, and the other places in Cairo and Antwerp. You know about Earless' father in Mexico City, don't you? Don't you?" His face is inches from Frieda's.

This isn't what I was afraid of. I was afraid he'd hurt me, not Frieda. But, you know, this version is worse. I try to look away, but I can't.

Frieda doesn't say anything. Her arms and legs are shaking.

I can't take it anymore. She's not the annoying rich kid I met on the plane. She's become a friend – at least a friend. And, dammit all, she has a disability. A large part of her life is tougher than most people's. I can feel my fear draining out of me, flushed away by another, stronger emotion. I'm not scared anymore. I'm mad. "Hey!" I say. "Put her down!"

Keeping hold of Frieda, Slouchy turns around to glare at me. "You're next," he says. Even now I'm not frightened.

Anger is an elephant in your bedroom. There's no room for other emotions.

"She didn't tell – I did," I say. My voice cracks. I hate it when that happens. "Customs and Excise are on their way. They'll be here soon. Now leave her alone, you bully!"

I can't make him put her down. But Sally can. She jumps up and bites him on the seat of the pants. He yells and drops Frieda. She falls like a sack, her legs splayed out in front of her. Sally and I run over together. I kneel down. Sally licks her face.

Slouchy stands over us, growling like a bear. He lifts his hand – and freezes.

There's a gun right against his ear. A big black pistol. On TV, they don't look so big. Veronica uses two hands to hold the gun. "Police," she says. "Step away from the kids, now, or I'll blow your head off."

18

I'd Have Shot Him, Dear

Surprised doesn't cover it. Was Adam surprised when he saw Eve? Who's this? he said, and where's my rib?

"You're the police?" I say to Veronica. My jaw hangs open.

Skinny shakes his head. "I don't believe it," he says.

Slouchy believes it. Her gun is in his ear. He backs away from us. She pushes him towards his cousin. "Now, both of you, lie on the floor," she says. "Facedown."

"You can't do this," says Skinny. "I work here. I'm a government employee."

"On the floor."

She doesn't shout, but she's got the tone of command. The flight attendant tone. Pass your trays forward. Do up your seat belts – now. And, of course, she's got the gun. The two men lie down on the floor.

"Don't move a muscle," she says, with a smile she doesn't mean at all.

Slouchy growls some more.

"You'll never get away with this," says Skinny. "I'm a respectable citizen. You can't prove anything."

"What do you mean? Didn't you just admit everything to these two kids? Even I didn't know about Earless' father in Mexico."

Skinny is silent.

I can't help thinking about Earless and his dad. Is the old man proud of his son? Is he interested in the pyramids too? Does he have both his ears?

Veronica reaches into her purse with her free hand, and pulls out a set of handcuffs. Skinny and Slouchy are lying end to end. Quickly she cuffs Slouchy's hand to Skinny's foot. Now neither of them can move.

I help Frieda back into her wheelchair. She doesn't thank me. She stares down at Slouchy.

"You kids are with the C & E team, aren't you," says Veronica. She doesn't take her eyes off the bad guys on the floor. "Where is Special Agent Libby?"

– *Coming,* says Norbert.

"Good," she says. I guess she thinks it's Frieda talking.

– *I phoned, to tell him where we were,* says Norbert.

"Huh?" She flicks a glance our way. At that moment Slouchy moves his free hand. But Frieda is watching him the way a cat watches a mouse hole. When he moves, she rolls herself forward, and Slouchy yells.

"Ow! Ow! Get off!"

It must hurt to have the full weight of a fourteen-year-old girl, and her wheelchair, on your hand. Frieda spins in her wheelchair, so that the big back wheel grinds into his hand. Then she rolls herself backward, off his hand. Her face is calm.

"Ow! Why did you do that?"

"You moved," says Frieda. "She told you not to move."

"I think you cracked a bone!"

"Good."

I can't help giggling. Hysteria, I suppose. Or relief. And then Earless bursts through the door, which swings wide, knocking Veronica against me. Knocking her gun from her hand onto the floor.

I stop giggling.

The man the NYPD and the Customs and Excise Bureau are looking for is disguised in a pilot's uniform, but he doesn't really look like a pilot. He's too worried. He's panting, as if he's run a hard race. There are sweat stains around the uniform collar. The jacket isn't a perfect fit. But it's Earless all right.

His eyes go wide, as he takes in the whole scene. I can see the whites of his eyes all around his dark pupils. He reaches for the gun.

Time stretches like warm silly putty, so that each second goes on and on. I hear a roaring in my ears. I see things very clearly: the sweat on Earless' face, the surprise on Veronica's. I see the gun. It's lying on its side in the middle of the room, spinning around and around, slower and slower, like the pointer on a board game, telling you whose turn it is. The gun points to me, then spins past me to Veronica, then Frieda, then Skinny, then Slouchy. It slows and slows and comes to rest pointing at Earless.

It's Earless' turn.

He stretches out his hand. Veronica moves towards the gun too, but he's nearer than she is. He's going to get there first. I can see it all happening, but I'm powerless to prevent it because I can't seem to move at all.

Everyone is shouting, but I can't understand what they are saying. The words just add to the roar in my ears.

Earless picks up the gun, and stands there, with the gun pointing down. He freezes with the gun pointing down. A cold wet nose is pressed against him, against the gun hand, the hand that smells of creosote.

And then I hear a voice, resonating high and powerfully – a voice from beyond time. My ears aren't quite back to normal, but I can make out the words.

– *We meet again, Professor Malchus.*

The gun hand trembles violently. "Norberto?" asks Earless. "Is it you?"

– *No. New York is full of talking dogs. Of course it's me.*

Norbert sounds so normal, so much like himself, that I find I can move again. Time is back to normal. Veronica frowns beside me. I notice Skinny, staring at Sally in horror.

"Why are you here, now?" asks Earless.

– *Well, Sally's here because of that smelly stuff on your hand. But I – Norberto – have come for a deeper purpose.*

"Do you . . . have you anything to say to me?" asks Earless.

– I do. It is time, Professor. I will keep my promise.

"Do you mean . . ."

– I am ready to tell you the truth about the pyramids.

"Really?" Earless sounds fervent and excited, as if he's wished upon a star and had his wish come true. "Do you mean it?" he says.

– Yes. But you must put down the gun.

"I have to get out of here. My plane is leaving."

Veronica is staring at me like she can't believe it. "Is that you talking, kid?" she whispers.

– The triangular sides of the great pyramids directly face the points of the compass, and slope upwards at an angle of 50 degrees to meet at an apex. You know this. But do you know why the entrance to a pyramid is always through a northern wall?

"Why?" asks Earless.

– Put down the gun, and I'll tell you. Norberto means you no harm. And, for what it's worth, I don't think Sally will bite. The reason for the northern exposure is simple: the Cocoa Jug was visible in the north part of the Egyptian sky. Well, it used to be. It's moved.

"The Cocoa Jug?" says Earless.

– You don't know? The Jug is the most important constellation in the sky of Jupiter.

"Jupiter?"

– Come on, man. The Great Pyramid of Cheops is a solid mass of limestone blocks 756 feet square and 482 feet high. Could

you earthlings build that with your hammers and chisels? The power came from Jupiter.

"An alien race?" His mouth is open.

Slouchy is trying to scramble to his feet. He's having trouble because Skinny won't move. He has his hands over his ears. "Boss!" says Slouchy. "Boss!"

"Quiet, Andrews!" says Earless.

"But, boss!"

"Alien engineering is a theory, of course. Von Himmelhurst . . ."

– *Theory? My uncle was* there. *He convinced the pharaohs to put up pyramids in the first place. The early pharaohs were – well, put it this way. They wanted to dig holes in the ground, and throw in all their worldly goods. Can you believe it? The Great Holes of Egypt! Not exactly one of your Seven Wonders of the World! I tell you, Professor, these guys didn't even know what a pyramid was. Uncle Nathan had to tell them.*

Norbert is completely convincing. He makes it sound like it really happened that way. Earless is persuaded. "Egyptian gods from Jupiter! But this is amazing! Simply amazing! I have to write it down. Do you mind, Norberto?"

He puts the gun in his blue coat pocket and takes out a pad.

– *Of course not. I can tell you lots more about the Egyptian civilization. The people didn't always worship scarab beetles, you know. No, sir. It wasn't until Uncle Nathan crashed his spaceship right into the pharaoh's hat, and everyone thought he was a bug. Poor Uncle: millions of miles away from the nearest garage. . . .*

Earless hardly notices when Special Agent Libby and the police escort charge through the door. His attention is all on the dog. "Go on," he says.

"You have the right to remain silent," says Libby.

"Not you," says Earless. "Go on about scarabs, Norberto."

"You have the right to consult an attorney," continues Libby. "If you cannot afford an attorney, one will be appointed for you. . . ."

Skinny is protesting. "Why am I in handcuffs?" he asks. "Don't you realize that I'm a government employee?" He says something about hearsay evidence, and his word against ours. Veronica takes a tiny tape recorder from her jacket pocket, and puts it into an evidence bag, and Skinny's face goes white, and he refuses to say anything more until he talks to a lawyer. He and Slouchy are led away under guard. One of Slouchy's shirtsleeves is ripped. I notice a tattoo on his arm: a heart with a dagger stuck in it. On the heart is the name BETTY. Not ungross.

Special Agent Libby shakes my hand, and pats Sally on the head. Frieda gets a handshake too. "You did great," he tells her.

"Even though I'm . . . a girl?" she says.

"You're quite a girl," he says. "Sorry we took so long to get here," he tells Veronica, who turns out to be a detective sergeant with the New York City Fraud Squad. "We were held up by that movie. Thanks for calling to tell us where you were. I didn't know you had my cell phone number."

"I don't have it," she says. "I check in through dispatch."

There's a pause. They frown at each other. "Well, whatever," says the agent.

I look around for Bird, but he isn't there.

Frieda rolls herself over to Detective Sergeant Veronica. "So you were working for the police all along," she says. "Even on the plane?"

"Yes, dear," says Veronica. "Customs and Excise have been trying to get a pipeline into Earless' smuggling racket for a long time now. I'd done some flight attending before I joined the police, and I volunteered for the assignment."

"Why did you disappear this morning?" I ask.

"I was afraid of being recognized. One of my precinct officers was on duty – a nice guy, but not the brightest light in the chandelier, if you know what I mean. In fact, I sometimes think his dog Lucky is smarter than he is."

"And in the alley?" says Frieda. "You drove away and left us."

"I phoned in your location as soon as I could. The police are still combing the neighborhood, unless someone remembered to call them off."

"Oh. Thank you."

"You're welcome."

Frieda takes a deep breath. "And just now. When . . . he was holding me up against the wall. . . ." She shudders, thinking back.

"I wanted Andrews to keep talking. Every word he said was evidence. I wouldn't have let him hurt you."

"But . . . he did hurt me. Holding me up like that. My shoulder is still sore. And he scared me to death." Her mom comes over now, and puts her hand on her daughter's shoulder.

Sergeant Veronica looks uncomfortable. "I did what I thought was best," she says. "It was a dangerous situation you two stumbled into."

And she is right about that.

"What if he was actually going to hurt me?" Frieda asks.

"I'd have shot him, dear." Veronica turns away to accept some more congratulations.

Mrs. Miller gasps. Is Frieda satisfied? I don't know. I feel sick.

The dog is scratching at the inside door.

19

I Hate This Military Time

C & E holds a press conference at the entrance to the airport. Lights, cameras, reporters. Special Agent Libby answers most of the questions, but there are enough newspaper and TV people to interview everyone. They even interview me, though my questions are all about Frieda.

"Is Representative Miller's daughter an inspiration to you?" one reporter asks me.

"I dunno," I say. "More a friend, I guess."

I reach up to adjust my sunglasses. I'm wearing them against the glare of the TV lights.

"What does her disability mean to you?"

"I dunno," I say. "Not much. It probably means more to her."

"How do you see yourself, in relation to Frieda?"

"Sometimes beside her, talking," I answer, "and sometimes behind her, helping to push."

"That was Alan Dingman, ladies and gentlemen," says the reporter.

"Dingwall," I say.

A man walks through the sliding doors. A tall rangy fellow with a rugged cowboy face, and his suit coat flung over his shoulder. Frieda's whole body gets a jolt of electricity when she sees him. Her face lights up with joy. Dropping Sally's leash, she cries, "Daddy! Daddy!" and wheels herself forward.

Her dad makes it to the airport, but mine doesn't. For a moment, I can't look at her.

"Hey, there!" he says. I'm holding the leash. I can look now. He's kneeling beside her chair, smiling. A nice deep voice, and wet white teeth. He turns her around so they can both smile at the cameras. "Now, what have you been up to? I thought your flight wasn't due in yet."

"My flight got in this morning," she says.

"And what's this press conference about? Customs and Excise? I heard about it in my office, and dashed right over. My little girl is a hero!"

"Oh, Daddy!"

Reporters surge around his rugged profile like angry waves beating on a rockbound coast. He smiles for them all. When he notices his wife, his smile flashes off in surprise, then back on again, bigger and whiter than ever. "Gladys! This is great. Just great. Come on over, honey." Mrs. Miller joins her husband and daughter, and the three of them pose in front of the cameras.

– So, how have you enjoyed your day in the big city? Has it been Sid enough for you?

I hesitate. I was going to say it's been awful, every minute, but it hasn't. Looking back, there's been stuff to enjoy, to savor, to laugh at. The picture of Norberto rising from the sarcophagus is etched forever in my memory. "It's been a real adventure," I say. "So far." The problem is, the day still isn't over. "But what's going to happen now?" I ask.

– Well, I thought I'd put on a pot of cocoa, and give Nerissa a call. There's a lot to catch up on.

"I mean, what's going to happen to me?" I say. "You're going to go to Frieda's house, and I'll be all alone."

– I thought you wanted to be independent.

"I don't want to be all alone," I say.

– You aren't. You never are.

"This is the dog I told you about. And the boy."

Frieda's father pushes the wheelchair. Mom trails behind, dutifully.

"Hello," I say.

"Hello, young man." A firm handclasp and sincere smile for me, then he passes by me and drops my hand. He and his smile move on to Sally.

"A good-looking dog," he says.

"And we can keep her? You weren't kidding?" Frieda sounds a bit doubtful, as if there have been other times when her dad was supposed to do things, and didn't do them, and claimed that he'd been kidding all along.

"Sure," he says.

"How not uncool! Thanks, Daddy!"

"My campaign manager will be happy – he's been after me to get a dog. Did you know that sixty-four percent of registered voters in the state of New York like dogs?"

The state representative doesn't look at us while he's talking. He looks all around, all the time. He's keeps turning the wheelchair to point at one of the cameras.

"I'm glad you came, Daddy," says Frieda.

"Thanks, honey. Anything for you. Wait – there's Cam Christie from the *Post*. I must just go and say hello. Let me bring the dog. What'd you say her name was?"

"Sally," says Frieda, with a sigh.

"Perfect." He straightens his tie. "Come on, Sally."

Half an hour later it's 17:55 by the airport TV screens. 5:55 by my watch. I'm standing in front of the airport LOST AND FOUND office, clutching my Commodores soccer bag.

The press conference is over. Police and reporters and cameras are gone. So is Frieda's dad, who remembered important business back at the office, kissed his wife and daughter, patted the dog, and jumped in a limousine. Is Frieda disappointed? She doesn't seem to be. Maybe she's used to it. Her mom has her hand on Frieda's shoulder. That may be something she isn't used to. But I bet she can get used to it.

Frieda's suitcase isn't in the LOST AND FOUND. "Maybe someone mailed it to you," I say. "Maybe someone saw your address printed on the luggage tag, and mailed your suitcase to the house."

Frieda laughs. So does the lady in charge of the LOST AND FOUND. Even Mrs. Miller finds a smile for the hayseed from out of town.

I don't feel much like smiling myself. I've phoned Frieda's place three or four times, using Mrs. Miller's cell phone. No word from Dad.

My soccer bag looks exactly the same as it did this morning. Exactly the same as it did a few weekends ago, when I took it to Victor's cottage on Rice Lake. I can't help wondering if I look any different. I feel different.

"I'm sorry your father's late," says Mrs. Miller. "I'm sure there's a perfectly normal explanation."

"Yeah," I say.

"Well, I suppose we'd best be getting back for dinner."

"Alan's coming back with us, isn't he?" says Frieda. "We can't just leave him here. You can stay to dinner with us, can't you, Alan?"

"Sure," I say. Where else do I have to go?

Back on the moving sidewalk, on our way out, Frieda and her mom are having an intimate conversation. I don't want to listen, but I can't help hearing. "Remember what the therapist said? It would be natural for you to blame me." Mrs. Miller puts her hand on her daughter's shoulder. "I guess that's the reason I'm afraid of you."

"But why would I blame you?"

"For letting you down. For somehow making you the way you are."

"You're my mom. You brought me into the world."

A medium-sized guy steps on one moving sidewalk as we step off the other. He's going into the airport as we're going out. He is unremarkable in almost every way, except for the red hair, which is just starting to turn gray around the temples.

"Dad!" I say.

I drop my bag and almost fall down. Sudden weakness in the knees. Dad steps off the moving sidewalk and strolls towards me. "Hey, champ!" he says. "Great to see you. Nice shades. Been waiting long?"

He looks so incredibly normal. Not tired or strained. Not ecstatic. His suit is buttoned. His hair is combed. His leather shoes gleam. He reminds me of my soccer bag – nothing has really changed about him since the last time I saw him. He's pleased to see me, and that's all. Has he been running around the city, frantic with worry? He has not. Are his knees weak, now that we've finally found each other? Bet not. "Your plane was early, then," he says.

I don't say anything. I can't. I want to say something not uncool, but I just can't.

He holds out his hand. I take it because what else am I going to do?

"Where . . . oh, Daddy, where have you been?" I say. Uncool. Damn.

"What do you mean? Your plane isn't due in for almost another hour. I didn't want to miss it, so I cut my last meeting short and hurried over. How about that – I'm forty-five minutes early for something. Your mom won't believe it." He's still smiling. He doesn't get it. He has no idea of what has been going on.

Mrs. Miller takes over. "Alan flew to New York with my daughter."

"That's great. Nice to meet you, Mrs. . . ."

"Miller. Gladys Miller. My husband is . . . I mean, my daughter is named Frieda."

"Nice to meet both of you." Dad shakes hands. His smile isn't forced or strained. "So, why was the plane so early? Tailwinds or something? My schedule has you arriving at 18:45. That's, what, quarter to seven. Gee, I hate this military time."

He holds out an official-looking piece of paper. I practically tear it from his hand, to see the time. 18:45, all right. "There was a mistake," I say. "It should say 8:45."

Dad shakes his head. "No, champ. That can't be right. You haven't been here since 8:45 this morning, have you?"

He stares at me and Frieda.

"Oh, champ. Oh, buddy boy. How awful. I'm so sorry. Hanging around an airport for ten hours. Your day must have been so boring."

There's a pause. I find myself giving my dad a quirky little smile. "No," I say, finally. "It wasn't boring."

Me and Bruce Willis. Only I'm not in a movie. This is my life.

Afterword

Two Months Later

My dad and I did stay in a hotel, and order room service, and it was not uncool. We got to a baseball game the night before I came home, and I went to the bathroom by myself in the fourth inning. And I took my time. When I got back to my seat, Dad was looking a bit anxious. I smiled.

He went with me to the airport, and let me pick a souvenir gift. It was an easy choice. Sleek, black, palm-sized, with four functions including speed dial.

I survived the plane trip back to Toronto. Mom met me at the Toronto airport, and made me write my dad a card to thank him for an exciting vacation. He hasn't written back yet.

School starts next week. Grade eight – am I ready? My new teacher is Mr. Reynolds, an old man who wears zippered cardigans and yells all the time. I used to be frightened of him. Now I don't know. His gray hair is natural. And he doesn't wear cologne.

I talk to Frieda fairly often. Having my own cell phone makes a difference. Apparently Mrs. Miller has quit the Tutankhamen Society and Sally has turned the sarcophagus into her own doghouse. Frieda talks about Sally all the time, but doesn't mention Norbert. I wonder if he's still there. I'd call him up if I knew the number.

Frieda's got another operation scheduled in Toronto around Christmastime. Maybe we'll get together. Last week she sent me an article from *Discovery* magazine. The author, Dr. Malchus, is described as a noted expert in the field of Egyptology, currently awaiting trial. The article is titled: "The Truth about the Great Pyramids." I haven't read it yet.

I got a postcard from Bird in today's mail. He's having a wonderful time, and feels right at home where he is. I don't know where that is, exactly. There's no stamp or postmark on the card. The picture on the front is of a little baby sleeping on its mother's stomach.

From *The Nose from Jupiter*:

I started to sneeze. I sneezed and sneezed and sneezed. Finally, about twenty sneezes later, I stopped. I couldn't feel anything. I sniffed a few times, experimentally. Still no feeling.

Fine. I must have dislodged the . . . whatever it was. I went back to the lawn mower. That's when I heard the voice.

– *Here we are at last*, it said.

I looked over my shoulder to see who was talking, but somehow I knew there wasn't anyone there. The squeaky voice was coming from inside me. Inside my nose.

– *Ah, this is nice. Say, this is a great place you've got here.*

"Hello," I said. "Who are you?"

– *Living room, bedroom, kitchen, back room. And a garage, of course. Very nice indeed. I think I'm going to be happy here.*

"What are you talking about?" I said.

– *If you could see the place I was living on Jupiter, this . . . this is luxury. Just like the commercials you people send out. This is the life. Ah.*

"That's my nose you're talking about," I said. "Isn't it?"

– *You tell me. I'm a stranger here myself.*

A high and squeaky voice, coming from inside my nose.